G.K. CHESTERTON
Daylight and Nightmare

Uncollected Stories and Fables

SELECTED AND ARRANGED BY

Marie Smith

Dodd, Mead & Company · New York

First published in the United States in 1986

Contents copyright © Miss D.E. Collins
This Selection and Foreword © Marie Smith 1986

Published by Dodd, Mead & Company, Inc.
79 Madison Avenue, New York, N.Y. 10016
Distributed in Canada by
McClelland and Stewart Limited, Toronto

First Edition
First published in Great Britain by
Xanadu Publications Limited, 1986

Library of Congress Cataloging in Publication Data

Chesterton, G.K. (Gilbert Keith), 1874 – 1936.
   Daylight and Nightmare
   I. Title
PR4453.C4D3   1986   823'.912   86-16593
ISBN 0-396-08889-9

Foreword

It is a great pleasure to be able to bring together in one volume the best of G.K. Chesterton's uncollected stories, which span a period from the 1890s, when as a boy at St Paul's School he was making his first attempts at serious fiction (and some of it is very serious indeed), to the fables that he wrote anonymously for *G.K.'s Weekly* in the late 1920s, towards the end of his life. Although a few of these stories have appeared in anthologies, they are 'uncollected' in the sense that they were never included in any of Chesterton's own books of collected fiction, and the others have never appeared in book form at all. I have arranged them in three chronological groups, representing the three main phases of Chesterton's career — his beginnings, when he was a student at the Slade School; his mature work as a writer and journalist, from roughly 1906 to 1914; and his post-war writings, mostly for his own journal, *G.K.'s Weekly*. The shorter fables from this last period are, however, interspersed throughout.

All the stories are fantasies of one sort or another. From the outset, Chesterton was prepared to tackle ambitious themes, and the stories in the first part of the book reflect, in fantastic form, his adolescent concerns. At the Slade, surrounded by juvenile manifestations of Decadence, he believed himself to be going mad and had to fight a tremendous battle to free himself of his own morbid thoughts, which were dominated by images of cruelty and violence. That he succeeded is unremarkable; most adolescents do. But the manner in which he did it was strange, taking the form of a sort of willed optimism which expressed itself in a new-found delight in the world; literally, an awakening. 'A Crazy Tale', written at precisely this time, is an assertion of this awakening process, and the other stories from the period are similarly revealing. I have grouped them together under the heading 'A Sense of Wonder', which I think describes Chesterton's state of mind at the time.

Yet even when he seemed to be writing in the highest of high spirits, horrors were never far away. It was something of which Chesterton himself was only too well aware:

A sunset of copper and gold had just broken down and gone to pieces in the west, and grey colours were crawling over everything in earth and heaven; also a wind was growing, a wind that laid a cold finger upon flesh and spirit. The bushes at the back of my garden began to whisper like conspirators; and then to wave like wild hands in signal... A black flapping thing detaches itself from one of the sombre trees and flutters to another. I know not if it is owl or flittermouse; I could fancy it was a black cherub of darkness, not with the wings of a bird and the head of a baby, but with the head of a goblin and the wings of a bat. I think, if there were light enough, I could sit here and write some very creditable creepy tale, about how I went up the crooked road beyond the church and met Something — say a dog, a dog with one eye. Then I should meet a horse, perhaps a horse without a rider; the horse also would have one eye. Then the inhuman silence would be broken; I should meet a man (need I say, a one-eyed man?) who would ask me the way to my own house. Or perhaps tell me that it was burnt to the ground. I think I could tell a very cosy little tale along some such lines. Or I might dream of climbing for ever the tall dark trees above me. They are so tall that I feel as if I should find at their tops the nests of the angels; but in this mind they would be dark and dreadful angels; angels of death.

*   *   *

Only, you see, this mood is all bosh. I do not believe in it in the least. That one-eyed universe, with its one-eyed men and beasts, was only created by one universal wink. At the top of the tragic trees I should not find the Angel's Nest. I should only find the Mare's Nest; the dreamy and divine nest is not there. In the Mare's Nest I shall discover that dim, enormous opalescent egg from which is hatched the Nightmare. For there is nothing so delightful as a nightmare — when you know it is a nightmare...

*   *   *

Therefore I see no wrong in riding with the Nightmare tonight; she winnies to me from the rocking tree-tops and the roaring wind; I will catch her and ride her through the awful air. Woods and weeds are alike tugging at the roots in the rising tempest, as if all wished to fly with us over the moon, like that wild amorous cow whose child was the Moon-Calf. We will rise to that mad infinite where there is neither up nor down, the high topsy-turveydom of the heavens. I will answer the call of chaos and old night. I will ride on the Nightmare; but she shall not ride on me.

The same idea is given a literal manifestation in a story included here, 'The Taming of the Nightmare' — with equally unconvincing protestations as to who is riding whom. Jorge Luis Borges, in one of his brief but characteristically penetrating essays, goes straight to the heart of the matter:

Chesterton would not have tolerated the imputation of being a contriver of nightmares, a *monstrorum artifex* (Pliny, XXVIII), but he tends inevitably to revert to atrocious observations. He asks if perchance a man has three eyes, or a bird three wings; in opposition to the pantheists, he speaks of a man who dies and discovers in paradise that the spirits of the angelic choirs have, every one of them, the same face he has; he speaks of a jail of mirrors; of a labyrinth without a centre; of a man devoured by metal automatons;

of a tree that devours birds and then grows feathers instead of leaves; he imagines (*The Man Who Was Thursday*, VI) 'that if a man went westward to the end of the world he would find something — say a tree — that was more or less than a tree, a tree possessed by a spirit; and that if he went east to the end of the world he would find something else that was not wholly itself — a tower, perhaps, of which the very shape was wicked'...

These examples, which could easily be multiplied, prove that Chesterton restrained himself from being Edgar Allan Poe or Franz Kafka, but something in the makeup of his personality leaned towards the nightmarish, something secret, and blind, and central... That discord, that precarious subjection of a demoniacal will, defines Chesterton's nature.

By 1906, Chesterton was finding his way as an author and journalist (although we are still a long way from his conversion to Catholicism), and the stories from this period are correspondingly more mature, written in a style that has become both more polished and more detached. The arguments, the paradoxes and the horrors are all offered in a jolly, throw-away style that is at once disarming and disturbing; it is difficult to think of any other writer who could create the appalling image of the Superman, and yet manage to tell the story more or less as a joke. The ability to create monsters is by no means a negligible one, and if Chesterton's were born of conflict, they acquire power because of it. Deliberately striving for such effects generally produces lamentable results, as in the case of H.P. Lovecraft (to take an extreme example).

After the war — and after the death of his brother and his own subsequent collapse — the character of Chesterton's writing changed. He was moving steadily towards Catholicism, but was horribly overworked in trying to maintain *G.K.'s Weekly* as well as keeping up an enormous volume of other writing, and the strain shows. Some of his light-heartedness vanishes, his tales begin to acquire a rather grimly polemic purpose, and the writing itself is much more careless. From this later output I have therefore selected very sparingly. The liveliest of the fables (the 'Tops' from the 'Top and Tail' page of *G.K.'s Weekly*) are here, together with two stories ('Concerning Grocers as Gods' and 'The Paradise of Human Fishes') from a series called *Utopias Unlimited* that unfortunately never reached Episode Three — it would perhaps have made a pleasant book somewhat along the lines of *The Club of Queer Trades* — plus some other stray items.

The best of Chesterton's fictional writing, which I would take to include *The Man Who Was Thursday*, the finest of the Father Brown stories, and some of the tales included here, is unlike anything else that has been written before or since, a delight to those who can rejoice in a strong intellect at play, and a lively sense of the fantastic and the bizarre. One could point to other virtues — the great skill with which a scene is set in broad, impressionist strokes, or the extraordinary range of grotesque characters — or to his key influence on other writers (as diverse as Kafka, McLuhan, Tolkien and, of course, Borges himself), but the task of revaluating Chesterton must wait a while longer, and at this point the stories must speak for themselves. They will not appeal to everyone; to quote an experience related by C.S. Lewis:

> A lady (and, what makes the story more piquant, she herself was a Jungian psychologist by profession) had been talking a dreariness which seemed to be creeping over her life, the drying up in her of the power to feel pleasure, the aridity of her mental landscape. Drawing a bow at a venture, I asked, 'Have you any taste for fantasies and fairy tales?' I shall never forget how her muscles tightened, her hands clenched themselves, her eyes started as if with horror, and her voice changed, as she hissed out, 'I *loathe* them.' Clearly we here have to do not with a critical opinion but with something like a phobia.

— but for the rest of us, here are riches indeed. In the words of Borges, who sadly died as this book was going to press, and to whose memory I respectfully dedicate it:

> Literature is one of the forms that happiness takes; perhaps no writer has given me as many happy hours as Chesterton.

—Marie Smith

Contents

PART ONE

A Sense of Wonder

PART TWO

From the Land of Nightmare

PART THREE

Utopias Unlimited

Introductory: On Gargoyles

Alone at some distance from the wasting walls of a disused abbey I found half sunken in the grass the grey and goggle-eyed visage of one of those graven monsters that made the ornamental water-spouts in the cathedrals of the Middle Ages. It lay there, scoured by ancient rains or striped by recent fungus, but still looking like the head of some huge dragon slain by a primeval hero. And as I looked at it, I thought of the meaning of the grotesque, and passed into some symbolic reverie of the three great stages of art.

I

Once upon a time there lived upon an island a merry and innocent people, mostly shepherds and tillers of the earth. They were republicans, like all primitive and simple souls; they talked over their affairs under a tree, and the nearest approach they had to a personal ruler was a sort of priest or white witch who said their prayers for them. They worshipped the sun, not idolatrously, but as the golden crown of the god whom all such infants see almost as plainly as the sun.

Now this priest was told by his people to build a great tower, pointing to the sky in salutation of the Sun-god; and he pondered long and heavily before he picked his materials. For he was resolved to use nothing that was not almost as clear and exquisite as sunshine itself; he would use nothing that was not washed as white as the rain can wash the heavens, nothing that did not sparkle as spotlessly as that crown of God. He would have nothing grotesque or obscure; he would not have even anything emphatic or even anything mysterious. He would have all the arches as light as laughter and as candid as logic. He built the temple in three concentric courts, which were cooler and more exquisite in substance each than the other. For the outer wall was a hedge of white lilies, ranked so thick that a green stalk was hardly to be seen; and the wall within that was of crystal, which smashed the sun into a million stars. And the wall within that, which was the tower itself, was a tower of pure water, forced up in an everlasting fountain; and upon the very tip and crest of that foaming

11

spire was one big and blazing diamond, which the water tossed up eternally and caught again as a child catches a ball.

"Now", said the priest, "I have made a tower which is a little worthy of the sun."

II

But about this time the island was caught in a swarm of pirates; and the shepherds had to turn themselves into rude warriors and seamen; and at first they were utterly broken down in blood and shame; and the pirates might have taken the jewel flung up for ever from their sacred fount. And then, after years of horror and humiliation, they gained a little and began to conquer because they did not mind defeat. And the pride of the pirates went sick within them after a few unexpected foils; and at last the invasion rolled back into the empty seas and the island was delivered. And for some reason after this men began to talk quite differently about the temple and the sun. Some, indeed, said, "You must not touch the temple; it is classical; it is perfect, since it admits no imperfections." But the others answered, "In that it differs from the sun, that shines on the evil and the good and on mud and monsters everywhere. The temple is of the noon; it is made of white marble clouds and sapphire sky. But the sun is not always of the noon. The sun dies daily; every night he is crucified in blood and fire."

Now the priest had taught and fought through all the war, and his hair had grown white, but his eyes had grown young. And he said, "I was wrong and they are right. The sun, the symbol of our father, gives life to all those earthly things that are full of ugliness and energy. All the exaggerations are right, if they exaggerate the right thing. Let us point to heaven with tusks and horns and fins and trunks and tails so long as they all point to heaven. The ugly animals praise God as much as the beautiful. The frog's eyes stand out of his head because he is staring at heaven. The giraffe's neck is long because he is stretching towards heaven. The donkey has ears to hear — let him hear."

And under the new inspiration they planned a gorgeous cathedral in the Gothic manner, with all the animals of the earth crawling over it, and all the possible ugly things making up one common beauty, because they all appealed to the god. The columns of the temple were carved like the necks of giraffes; the dome was like an ugly tortoise; and the highest pinnacle was a monkey standing on his head and his tail pointing at the sun. And yet the whole was beautiful, because it was lifted up in one living and religious gesture as a man lifts his hands in prayer.

III

But this great plan was never properly completed. The people had brought up on great wagons the heavy tortoise roof and the huge necks of stone, and all the thousand and one oddities that made up that unity, the owls and the efts and the crocodiles and the kangaroos, which hideous by themselves might have been magnificent if reared in one definite proportion and dedicated to the sun. For this was Gothic, this was romantic, this was Christian art; this was the whole advance of Shakespeare upon Sophocles. And that symbol which was to crown it all, the ape upside down, was really Christian; for man is the ape upside down.

But the rich, who had grown riotous in the long peace, obstructed the thing, and in some squabble a stone struck the priest on the head and he lost his memory. He saw piled in front of him frogs and elephants, monkeys and giraffes, toadstools and sharks, all the ugly things of the universe which he had collected to do honour to God. But he forgot why he had collected them. He could not remember the design or the object. He piled them all wildly into one heap fifty feet high; and when he had done it all the rich and influential went into a passion of applause and cried, "This is real art! This is Realism! This is things as they really are!"

*   *   *

That, I fancy, is the only true origin of Realism. Realism is simply Romanticism that has lost its reason. This is so not merely in the sense of insanity but of suicide. It has lost its reason; that is its reason for existing. The old Greeks summoned godlike things to worship their god. The mediaeval Christians summoned all things to worship theirs, dwarfs and pelicans, monkeys and madmen. The modern realists summon all these million creatures to worship their god; and then have no god for them to worship. Paganism was in art a pure beauty; that was the dawn. Christianity was a beauty created by controlling a million monsters of ugliness; and that in my belief was the zenith and the noon. Modern art and science practically mean having the million monsters and being unable to control them; and I will venture to call that the disruption and the decay. The finest lengths of the Elgin marbles consist of splendid horses going to the temple of a virgin. Christianity, with its gargoyles and grotesques, really amounted to saying this: that a donkey could go before all the horses of the world when it was really going to the temple. Romance means a holy donkey going to the temple. Realism means a lost donkey going nowhere.

The fragments of futile journalism or fleeting impression which are here collected are very like the wrecks and riven blocks that were piled in a heap round my imaginary priest of the sun. They are very like that grey and gaping head of stone that I found overgrown with the grass. Yet I will venture to make even of these trivial fragments the high boast that I am a mediaevalist and not a modern. That is, I really have a notion of why I have collected all the nonsensical things there are. I have not the patience nor perhaps the constructive intelligence to state the connecting link between all these chaotic papers. But it could be stated. This row of shapeless and ungainly monsters which I now set before the reader does not consist of separate idols cut out capriciously in lonely valleys or various islands. These monsters are meant for the gargoyles of a definite cathedral. I have to carve the gargoyles, because I can carve nothing else; I leave to others the angels and the arches and the spires. But I am very sure of the style of the architecture and of the consecration of the church.

PART ONE
A Sense of
Wonder

A Crazy Tale

"Hey, diddle, diddle,
The cat and the fiddle,
The cow jumped over the moon."

It is incredible, but true, that a young man sat opposite me in a restaurant and spoke as is hereafter set down.

He was a tall, spare man, carefully dressed in a formal frock-coat and silk hat. His tone was low and casual, his manner simple and very slow, and his bleak blue eyes never changed. Anyone just out of earshot of the words would have supposed that he was describing, in a rather leisurely way, an opera or a cycling tour. I alone heard the words; and ever since that day I have gone about ready for the Apocalypse, expecting the news of some incalculable revolution in human affairs. For I know that we have reached a new era in the history of our planet: the creation of a second Adam.

He spoke as follows, between the puffs of a cigar:

"I do not ask anyone to believe this story. Only in some wild hour of a windy night, when we could believe anything, when the craziest of a knot of old wives is wiser than all the schools of reason, when the blood is lawless and the brain dethroned, when we could see the windmills grind the wind, and the sea drag the moon, the apple-tree grow lemons, and the cow lay eggs, as in a wild half-holiday of nature; then, in the ear and coarsely, let this tale be told.

"When my story begins, I was walking in a still green place. The words sound strange and abrupt even in my own ears; but there is a reason for their abruptness.

"At that point the record of my life breaks off. The day, hour, or second before some stunning blow, some tremendous event befell me, and I awoke without a memory.

"Of the lost knowledge thus sealed within me I have a kind of half-witted fear. I move trembling in the close proximity of something huge, yet hidden in the darkness of my brain. Only of two things I am convinced. The first is, that this event, which I cannot recall, was the greatest of my life; that all my after adventures, wild as they were, were dwarfed in its unapproachable presence. The second comes of a certain hour, when suddenly, and for a second, the veil was lifted and I knew all. It had gone in a flash, but I am profoundly convinced that if I tell to another all the circumstances that led up to that instantaneous revelation, to him also, as he studies them, the words will suddenly give up their meaning, and their simplicity strike him with an awful laughter.

"This, then, is the story.

"The greenness, that I walked like one in a dream, stretched away on all sides to the edges of the sky. Sleepily, I let my eyes fall and woke, with a stunning thrill, to clearness. I stood shrunken with the shock, clutching myself in the smallest compass.

"Every inch of the green place was a living thing, a spire or tongue, rooted in the ground for those fantastic armies. The silence deafened me with a sense of busy eating, working, and breeding. I thought of that multitudinous life, and my brain reeled.

"Treading fearfully amid the growing fingers of the earth, I raised my eyes, and at the next moment shut them, as at a blow. High in the empty air blazed and streamed a great fire, which burnt and blinded me every time I raised my eyes to it. I have lived many years under this meteor of a fixed Apocalypse, but I have never survived the feelings of that moment. Men eat and drink, buy and sell, marry, are given in marriage, and all the time there is something in the sky at which they cannot look. They must be very brave.

"Again, a little while after, as in one of the changes in a dream, I found myself looking at something standing in the fields, something which looked at first like a man, and then like two men, and then like two men joined, till, after dizzy turning and tramping round it like the searching of a maze, I found it was some great abortion of nature with two legs at each end, calmly cropping the grass under the staring sun. I have said that I ask no one to believe this story.

"So I travelled along a road of portents, like undeciphered parables. There was no twilight as in a dream; everything was clear cut in the sunlight, standing out in defiant plainness and infantile absurdity. All was in simple colours, like the landscape of a child's alphabet, but to a child who had not learnt the meaning.

"At one time I seemed to come to the end of the earth; to a place

where it fell into space. A little beyond, the land re-commenced, but
between the two I looked down into the sky. As I bent over I saw
another bending over under me, hanging head downwards in those
fallen heavens, a little child with round eyes. It was some strange mercy
of God assuredly that the child did not fall far into hopeless eternity."

The young man paused reflectively. I tried to say "a pool," but
the words would not come. I seemed to have forgotten it. I seemed
to have forgotten everything except his terrible blue eyes, big with
unsupportable significance. Then I realised that he was speaking again.
"I heard a great noise out of the sky, and I turned and saw a giant.
Stories and legends there are of those who, in the morning of the
world, strayed also into the borders of the land of giants. But it is
impossible for any tongue to utter the overpowering sense of anarchy
and portent felt in seeing so much of the landscape moving upon two
legs, of looking up and seeing a face like my own, colossal, filling
the heavens.

"He lifted me like a flying bird through space and set me upon
his shoulder. I shall never forget the sight of his huge bare features
growing larger as I came nearer to them; the sun shining on them
as they smiled and smiled; a sight to give one dreams."

The young man paused again. I seemed to feel the whole sane
universe of custom and experience slipping from me, and with an effort like a drowning man's I cried out desperately. "But it was a man
— it was your father."

He raised his eyebrows, as at a coincidence. "So they said," he
observed. "Do you know what it means?"

I found myself broken and breathless, as Job might have been, bat-
tered with the earthquake question of Omniscience.

He went on, smoking slowly.

"With the giant was a woman. When I saw her something stirred
within me like the memory of a previous existence. And after I had
lived some little while with them, I began to have an idea of what
the truth must be. Instead of killing me, the giant and giantess fed
and tended me like servants. I began to understand that in that lost
epic of adventures which led up to the greatest event of my life, I
must have done some great service for these good people. What it
was, I had, by a quaint irony, myself forgotten. But I loved to see

it shining with inscrutable affection in the woman's eyes like the secret of the stars. There are few things more beautiful than gratitude.

"One day, as I stood beside her knee, she spoke to me; but I was speechless. A new and dreadful fancy had me by the throat. The woman was smaller than before. The house was smaller: the ceiling was nearer. Heaven and earth, even to the remotest star, were closing in to crush me.

"The next moment I had realised the truth, fled from the house, and plunged into the thickets like a thing possessed. A disease of transformation too monstrous for nightmare had quickened within me. I was growing larger and larger whether I would or no.

"I rolled in the gravel, revolving wild guesses as to whether I should grow to fill the sky, a giant with my head in heaven, bewildered among the golden plumage of Cherubim. This, as a matter of fact, I never did.

"It will always fill me with awe to think that no sign or premonition gave me warning of what I saw next. I merely raised my eyes — and saw it.

"Within a few feet of me was kneeling one of my own size, a little girl with big blue eyes and hair black as crows.

"The landscape behind her was the same in every hedge and tree that I had left; yet I felt sure I had come into a new world.

"I had got to my feet and made her a kind of bow, looking a fantastic figure enough; but a red star came into her cheek.

" 'Why, you are quite nice,' she said.

"I looked at her enquiringly.

" 'They say you are the mad boy,' she said, 'who stares at everything. But I think I like them mad.'

"I said nothing. I only stood up straight, and thanked God for every turn of my rambling path through that elvish topsey-turveydom, which had led at length to this. Although I had not asked for a miracle in answer, two or three drops of clear water fell out of the open sky.

" 'There will be a storm,' cried the girl hastily.

"She seemed quite frightened of the dark that had come over the wood, and the shocks of sound that shook the sky now and again. This fear surprised me, for she had not seemed afraid of the grass.

"She seemed so broken with the noise and dark and driving rain that I put my arm round her. As I did so, something new came over

me: a feeling less alien, and disturbed, more responsible and strangely strong; as if I had inherited a trust and privilege. For the first time
I felt a kinship with the monstrous landscape; I knew that I had been
sent to the right place.

" 'You are very brave,' she said, as the deafening skies seemed bowed about us and shouting in our ears; 'Do you not hear it?'

" 'I hear the daisies growing,' I said.

"Her answer was lost in the thunder.

"We were miles further on before she said, 'But are you not mad?'

"I spoke; but it seemed as if another spoke in my ear.

" 'I am the first that ever saw in the world. Prophets and sages
there have been, out of whose great hearts came schools and churches. But I am the first that ever saw a dandelion as it is.'

"Wind and dark rain swept round, swathing in a cloud the place
of that awful proclamation."

The young man paused once more. Some one near me moved his
chair against mine. I remember with what a start I realised that I was
in a crowded room; not in a desert with an insane hermit.

"But you have not told me," I said, "of the great moment: when
you seemed to have discovered all."

"It is soon told," he said. "Ten years afterwards the girl and I stood
in one room together: we were man and wife. Other men and women
went in and out, all of my own stature. There were no more giants;
it was as though I had dreamed of them. I seemed to have come back
among my own people.

"Just then my wife, who was bending over a kind of couch, lifted
a coverlet, and I saw that for which, haply, I have been sent to this
fantastic borderland of things.

"It was a little human creature hardly bigger than a bird. And when
I saw it, I — knew everything. I knew what was the greatest event
of my life: the event I had forgotten."

I said "Being born" in a low voice.

I did not dare to look at his face.

The next consciousness I had was that he had risen to his feet, and
was putting on his gloves very carefully.

I sprang erect also and spoke quickly.

"What does it mean? Are you a man? What thing are you? Are

you a savage, or a spirit, or a child? You wear the dress and speak
the language of a cultivated pupil of this over-cultivated time: yet you
see everything as if you saw it for the first time. What does it mean?"

After a silence he spoke in his quiet way.

"Have you ever said some simple word over and over till it became
unmeaning, a scrap of an unknown tongue, till you seem to be opening and shutting your mouth with a cry like an animal's? So it is with
the great world in which we live: it begins familiar: it ends unfamiliar.
When first men began to think and talk and theorise and work the
world over and over with phrases and associations, then it was involved and fated, as a psychological necessity, that some day a creature
should be produced, corresponding to the twentieth pronunciation
of the word, a new animal with eyes to see and ears to hear; with an
intellect capable of performing a new function never before conceiv-
ed truly; thanking God for his creation. I tell you religion is in its
infancy; dervish and anchorite, Crusader and Ironside, were not
fanatical enough, or frantic enough, in their adoration. A new type
has arrived. You have seen it."

He moved towards the door. Then I noticed he had come to a stand-
still again, and was gazing at the floor apparently in deep thought.

"I have never understood them," he said. "Those two creatures
I see everywhere, stumping along the ground, first one and then the
other. I have never been content with the current explanation that
they were my feet."

And he passed out, still carefully buttoning his gloves.

I went back to the table and sat down. About four minutes after
he was gone I felt a kind of mental shock, like something resuming
its place in my brain.

It occurred to me that the man was mad. I am almost ashamed to
admit with what suddenness it came. For so long as I was in his
presence, I had believed him and his whole attitude to be sane, normal, complete, and that it was the rest, the whole human race, that
were half-witted, since the making of the world.

Homesick At Home

One, seeming to be a traveller, came to me and said, "What is the shortest journey from one place to the same place?"

The sun was behind his head, so that his face was illegible.

"Surely," I said, "to stand still."

"That is no journey at all," he replied. "The shortest journey from one place to the same place is round the world." And he was gone.

White Wynd had been born, brought up, married and made the father of a family in the White Farmhouse by the river. The river enclosed it on three sides like a castle: on the fourth side there were stables and beyond that a kitchen-garden and beyond that an orchard and beyond that a low wall and beyond that a road and beyond that a pinewood and beyond that a cornfield and beyond that slopes meeting the sky, and beyond that — but we must not catalogue the whole earth, though it is a great temptation. White Wynd had known no other home but this. Its walls were the world to him and its roof the sky.

This is what makes his action so strange.

In his later years he hardly ever went outside the door. And as he grew lazy he grew restless: angry with himself and everyone. He found himself in some strange way weary of every moment and hungry for the next.

His heart had grown stale and bitter towards the wife and children whom he saw every day, though they were five of the good faces of the earth. He remembered, in glimpses, the days of his toil and strife for bread, when, as he came home in the evening, the thatch of his home burned with gold as though angels were standing there. But he remembered it as one remembers a dream.

Now he seemed to be able to see other homes, but not his own. That was merely a house. Prose had got hold of him: the sealing of the eyes and the closing of the ears.

At last something occurred in his heart: a volcano; an earthquake; an eclipse; a daybreak; a deluge; an apocalypse. We might pile up colossal words, but we should never reach it.

Eight hundred times the white daylight had broken across the bare kitchen as the little family sat at breakfast. And the eight hundred and first time the father paused with the cup he was passing in his hand.

"That green cornfield through the window," he said dreamily, "shining in the sun. Somehow, somehow it reminds me of a field outside my own home."

"Your own home?" cried his wife. "This is your home."

White Wynd rose to his feet, seeming to fill the room. He stretched forth his hand and took a staff. He stretched it forth again and took a hat. The dust came in clouds from both of them.

"Father," cried one child. "Where are you going?"

"Home," he replied.

"What can you mean? This is your home. What home are you going to?"

"To the White Farmhouse by the river."

"This is it."

He was looking at them very tranquilly when his eldest daughter caught sight of his face.

"Oh, he is mad!" she screamed, and buried her face in her hands.

He spoke calmly. "You are a little like my eldest daughter," he said. "But you haven't got the look, no, not the look which is a welcome after work."

"Madam," he said, turning to his thunderstruck wife with a stately courtesy. "I thank you for your hospitality, but indeed I fear I have trespassed on it too long. And my home —"

"Father, father, answer me! Is not this your home?"

The old man waved his stick.

"The rafters are cobwebbed, the walls are rain-stained. The doors bind me, the rafters crush me. There are littlenesses and bickerings and heartburnings here behind the dusty lattices where I have dozed too long. But the fire roars and the door stands open. There is bread and raiment, fire and water and all the crafts and mysteries of love. There is rest for heavy feet on the matted floor, and for starved heart in the pure faces, far away at the end of the world, in the house where I was born."

"Where, where?"

"In the White Farmhouse by the river."

And he passed out of the front door, the sun shining on his face.

And the other inhabitants of the White Farmhouse stood staring at each other.

White Wynd was standing on the timber bridge across the river, with the world at his feet.

And a great wind came flying from the opposite edge of the sky (a land of marvellous pale golds) and met him. Some may know what that first wind outside the door is to a man. To this man it seemed that God had bent back his head by the hair and kissed him on the forehead.

He had been weary with resting, without knowing that the whole remedy lay in sun and wind and his own body. Now he half believed that he wore the seven-leagued boots.

He was going home. The White Farmhouse was behind every wood and beyond every mountain wall. He looked for it as we all look for fairyland, at every turn of the road. Only in one direction he never looked for it, and that was where, only a thousand yards behind him, the White Farmhouse stood up, gleaming with thatch and whitewash against the gutsy blue of morning.

He looked at the dandelions and crickets and realised that he was gigantic. We are too fond of reckoning always by mountains. Every object is infinitely vast as well as infinitely small.

He stretched himself like one crucified in an uncontainable greatness.

"Oh God, who hast made me and all things, hear four songs of praise. One for my feet that Thou hast made strong and light upon Thy daisies. One for my head, which Thou hast lifted and crowned above the four corners of Thy heaven. One for my heart, which Thou hast made a heaven of angels singing Thy glory. And one for that pearl-tinted cloudlet far away above the stone pines on the hill."

He felt like Adam newly created. He had suddenly inherited all things, even the suns and stars.

Have you ever been out for a walk?

*   *   *

The story of the journey of White Wynd would be an epic. He was swallowed up in huge cities and forgotten: yet he came out on the other side. He worked in quarries, and in docks in country after country. Like a transmigrating soul, he lived a series of existences: a knot of vagabonds, a colony of workmen, a crew of sailors, a group of fishermen, each counted him a final fact in their lives, the great spare man with eyes like two stars, the stars of an ancient purpose.

But he never diverged from the line that girdles the globe.

On a mellow summer evening, however, he came upon the strangest thing in all his travels. He was plodding up a great dim down, that hid everything, like the dome of the earth itself.

Suddenly a strange feeling came over him. He glanced back at the waste of turf to see if there were any trace of boundary, for he felt like one who has just crossed the border of elfland. With his head a belfry of new passions, assailed with confounding memories, he toiled on the brow of the slope.

The setting sun was raying out a universal glory. Between him and it, lying low on the fields, there was what seemed to his swimming eyes a white cloud. No, it was a marble palace. No, it was the White Farmhouse by the river.

He had come to the end of the world. Every spot on earth is either the beginning or the end, according to the heart of man. That is the advantage of living on an oblate spheroid.

It was evening. The whole swell of turf on which he stood was turned to gold. He seemed standing in fire instead of grass. He stood so still that the birds settled on his staff.

All the earth and the glory of it seemed to rejoice round the madman's homecoming. The birds on their way to their nests knew him, Nature herself was in his secret, the man who had gone from one place to the same place.

But he leaned wearily on his staff. Then he raised his voice once more.

"O God, who hast made me and all things, hear four songs of praise. One for my feet, because they are sore and slow, now that they draw near the door. One for my head, because it is bowed and hoary, now that Thou crownest it with the sun. One for my heart, because Thou hast taught it in sorrow and hope deferred that it is the road that makes the home. And one for that daisy at my feet."

He came down over the hillside and into the pinewood. Through the trees he could see the red and gold sunset settling down among the white farm-buildings and the green apple-branches. It was his home now. But it could not be his home till he had gone out from it and returned to it. Now he was the Prodigal Son.

He came out of the pinewood and across the road. He surmounted the low wall and tramped through the orchard, through the kitchen garden, past the cattle-sheds. And in the stony courtyard he saw his wife drawing water.

Culture And The Light

The Traveller had the third-class railway carriage to himself all the way from London into the wilds of Yorkshire; dusk was already turning to dark upon the high wilderness of the moors; he had just taken out his cigar case to beguile the tedium with smoking, when the train slowed down at a wayside halt and the Stranger got into the carriage. The Stranger was grey of hair and garb, with certain oddities and even contradictions in his appearance: his shoulders were stooping, but his step light and springy, and his face was of the long sort called cadaverous, and associated with melancholy; yet he could often be seen to be secretly smiling. A few moments after the train had started again he leaned across and said politely, "Could you oblige me with a light?"

The Traveller immediately produced his match-box, and then hesitated a little, for his companion remained in the same polite posture, and showed no signs of producing anything to smoke.

"Excuse me," said the Traveller, "have you any tobacco? Or may I offer you a cigar?"

"Thank you," replied the other. "But I did not ask for a cigar; I only asked for a light."

Even as he spoke, the other had automatically struck a match and lit his own cigar. He was just about to toss away the match, when the Stranger made a sudden gesture as if seizing his wrist.

"For heaven's sake," he cried, "do not put it out yet! Why, it is not a third burnt through!"

The Traveller stared at the man, and began, for the first time, to be creepily conscious of the solitude and the stormy twilight. The flame of the match was in truth the only light in that world of shadow; and it lit the haggard face before him with an expression that was something more than fanatical. The man was still speaking.

"What waste! If you had thrown away the cigar and left the match burning — that would, at least, have been an ordinary, natural gesture. But to throw away the match and leave the cigar burning — what madness, what paradox, what perversity! Do you not remember in your holy childhood what a fairy transformation-scene it was to strike one of those little sticks of wood? And now you can buy boxes of them for twopence, bushels of them for a shilling, as if you were walking in a palace of fireworks. And then you will pay more to stick an ugly brown weed in your mouth and smell it!"

"Well," said the Traveller, humouring his lunatic, "the flame only lasts for a minute."

"It has lasted for ten thousand years," said the Stranger. "It will last till the planet freezes. It is your trumpery tobacco that has only lasted a few centuries among civilised men. And even then it depends on the fire. Fire has run through every religion; history has been a procession with torches; could it ever be a procession of cigars? What would be the good of a whole forest of cigars without the first spark of fire?"

"A smoker's inferno, I suppose," answered the other; "but some American millionaires chew unlighted cigars."

"I said among civilised men," said the Stranger; "but believe me, you have to choose between the old civilisation that can make fire and the new that can only manufacture cigars … Excuse me if I hold that match for a moment."

He took the flaming stump and held it tight, until his fingers seemed to shrink and blister with the heat.

"Should one not suffer a little," he asked calmly, "for having seen such glory?"

Perhaps the Traveller was a little relieved when he got out.

A Picture Of Tuesday

Oscar Plumtree was a rising artist, who painted his general impressions of his intimate friends, and belonged to a sketching club which met every Tuesday. He was a small square man with masses of black hair, and stood with his hands in his pockets, a little too conscious that his head was against a green curtain.

"How decorative Plumtree is," said Noel Starwood, symbolist, to Patrick Staunton, realist. "I never noticed that his colour was so arbitrary. But, like all the works of God, you have to see him twenty times before you see him for the first time."

"If you can suggest any course likely to result in seeing him for the last time," said Staunton, lighting a pipe, "I shall be more gratified. So he looks decorative, does he?"

"So flat," murmured Starwood, dreamily. "So admirably flat. He looks as if he had just come out of a panel by Albert Moor."

"Yes," said Staunton; "I wish he'd go back again."

Patrick Staunton was a large young man with a handsome passive face, that looked *blasé* but was only sleepy. He was very young, it is true, but not quite young enough to have grown weary of the world. He was, in fact, the average young man, with the average young man's two admirable qualities, a sense of humour and an aversion to egoists. This was why he disliked Plumtree. Noel Starwood, a slight, fiery-haired, fiery-tinted type, like a high-spirited girl, was a visionary, the painter of a series of 'Seven Dreams of Adam before the Creation of Eve.' He did not dislike Plumtree. He said it was the great test and trial of true Christian philosophy not to dislike Plumtree.

He moved off, and another member came up to Staunton.

"Do you know it is Plumtree's turn to give out a subject for the sketches?" he said. "These subject days are generally rather a lark. Do you remember the first time Starwood was asked for one? There was a silence, and then such a gentle, plaintive little voice said, 'The Resurrection of Cain.' But then he's a mystic, don't you know, and pities the Devil."

"Well, well," said Staunton charitably. "I heard Plumtree was going to the devil the other day and since then I rather pitied the devil myself.''

"But the joke of the thing is," continued the other,"that Plumtree is for ever telling us that the artistic mind cares no more for the subject of a picture, than for its weight in avoirdupois. He was immensely proud of his last picture, because three eminent art-critics looked at it the wrong way up.''

A small crowd had already gathered round Plumtree, and were pressing him for a subject.

"What do you want with a subject?" he said, contemptuously. "I don't want a subject, I want a picture. Won't anything do?''

"The primal enigma, Anything," said Starwood thoughtfully. "A fine conception. Something bizarre, hasty, fantastic. Some wild, low shape of life, to symbolise the germ-fact, the indestructible minimum, the everlasting Yea. After all, it is but a superficial philosophy which is founded on the existence of everything. The deeper philosophy is founded on the existence of anything.''

"Well, we won't have that," said Plumtree, abruptly. "You fellows don't seem to understand that art — ''

Staunton cut him short hastily. "I say, Plumtree, I asked for bread and you gave me a piece of india-rubber. Thanks. You were saying that the subject — ''

"Oh, take anything you like: what does the subject matter? What's the day of the week? Tuesday; very well." He turned to the throng and said in a clear voice, "The subject for the sketches will be Tuesday.''

"I beg your pardon," said Staunton politely.

"Tuesday," repeated Plumtree. "A picture of — Tuesday.''

Patrick Staunton lifted his full six feet two from the bench, and formally announced that he was relegated to a state of spiritual reprobation.

Only four members of the club exhibited sketches on this singular subject. The group consisted of Plumtree, Staunton and Starwood, and one Middleton, who had before him a lucrative career in virtue of an inexhaustible output of corpulent and comic monks.

The uncovering of his picture was received with loud cheers and laughter. It represented six monastic gentlemen of revolting joviality tossing pancakes. Thus it suggested Shrove Tuesday. Plumtree's was an admirable little suggestion of gaslight in early morning. It might just as well be Tuesday morning as any other morning.

Staunton annoyed him very much by elaborately describing the noble thoughts that the picture suggested to him. His own was a study of his mother's at-home day, which occurred on Tuesday, in which he introduced all the uncles who had told him things for his own good.

Starwood's picture was the largest. When it was unveiled it seemed to fill the room. It was a dark picture, dark with an intricate density of profound colours, a complex scheme of sombre and subtle harmonies, a kind of gorgeous twilight. Plumtree, who was far too good an artist to let cynicism rob him of the gift of wonder, followed the labyrinth of colour keenly and slowly.

Suddenly he gave a little cry and stepped back.

The whole was a huge human figure. Grey and gigantic, it rose with its back to the spectator. As far as the vast outline could be traced, he had one hand heaved above his head, driving up a load of waters, while below, his feet moved upon a solemn, infinite sea. It was a dark picture, but when grasped, it blinded like a sun.

Above it was written 'Tuesday,' and below, 'And God divided the waters that were under the firmament from the waters that were above the firmament: and the evening and the morning were the second day.'

There was a long silence, and Staunton was heard damning himself softly.

"It is certainly very good," he said, "like creation. But why did you reckon Tuesday the second instead of the third day of the Jewish week?"

"I had to reckon from my own seventh day: the day of praise, the day of saying 'It is good,' or I could not have felt it a reality."

"Do you seriously mean that you, yourself, look at the days of the week in that way?"

"The week is the colossal epic of creation," cried Starwood excitedly. "Why are there not rituals for every day? The Day of the Creation of Light, why is it not honoured with mystic illuminations? The Day of the Waters, why is it not the day of awful cleansings and sacred immersions — "

"Do you Transcendentalists only wash once a week?" asked Staunton.

"The Day of the Earth — what a fire of flowers and fruit; the Day of Birds, what a blaze of decorative plumage; the Day of Beasts, what a — "

"What a deed lot of nonsense," said Middleton, who was getting a trifle tired of all this. "If it comes to religion, and quotations from the Bible, what is there for us, Staunton? Can you think of a text for an at-home day?"

Staunton suggested, "And Job lifted up his voice and cursed his day."

But Plumtree was staring at the picture of Tuesday.

The Two Taverns

In the country of Old King Cole, the founder of the Colchester Oyster Feast, and therefore a distinguished diner-out, there were two partners who owned an inn called The Sun and Moon. One of them called Giles was rather loud and boastful, and the other called Miles rather silent and sarcastic; so that they soon quarrelled and set up opposition signs. That of Giles was called optimistically The Rising Sun, and that of Miles more modestly The Half Moon. There had been some dispute about the one barrel of sound wine they possessed; but at last it was drawn off into two smaller barrels in exactly equal quantities. It so happened that King Cole, with his celebrated Violin Orchestra and all his royal retinue, came riding from Colchester to the little village of London. He came first to the inn of The Rising Sun, with its beautiful groves of bushes festooned with coloured lights forming the legend: "Rising Sun Ruby Wine is the Best." Mr. Giles received the monarch with prostrations of hospitality, and took occasion to observe that the Ruby Wine sold at his establishment was the Best Wine in the World. And indeed the potentate had occasion to note that a similar opinion was inscribed on the flag flying from the turret, on the large blue bow decorating the dog, and that even the sardines and other *hors d'oeuvres* were arranged in patterns expressive of the same thought. When therefore the exuberant Giles had broken out for the sixth or seventh time into cries of admiring anticipation, touching the wine he intended to serve, the King, familiar by this time with the sentiment, suggested with some sharpness that the wine should be produced. His annoyance must be his excuse for the curious perversity which led him, even when the wine was produced, to say that he did not think so much of it after all. It must be remembered that he was a gentleman of the old school.

Leaving The Rising Sun, he resolved to push on to London, as there was evidently no other first-class hotel on the road; nothing but a shabby and unpretentious tavern called The Half Moon. At this, however, he consented to pause for a moment, his thirst having been greatly increased by the curious cookery of the superior hostel. "I am afraid," said Miles, the melancholy inkeeper, with an air of depression, "that there is really nothing in the house that is in the least fit to be offered to Your Majesty. We have a little cheap wine, but I fear you will think it the worst wine you ever drank in your life." "Not at all, not at all," said the King breezily. I assure you I know how to rough it." And he proceeded to give Miles somewhat misleading accounts of all he had gone through in his campaigns against the King of Chelmsford. And when the wine was served to him, he drank it with quite a roistering gesture and banged the goblet on the table, crying: "Blessed St. Julian, what uncommonly decent drink one can get in these little out-of-the-way places! Really, this stuff is quite excellent! I have indeed fallen on my feet."

This was not quite a correct figure of speech; he went on drinking the wine, and even attempted to dance with the village maidens; but it was not always on his feet that he fell.

The Taming of the Nightmare

Little Jack Horner sat in the corner — so far the traditional surroundings of the nursery hero correspond with those in which we find him for the purposes of the story, but there being no Christmas pie in the neighbourhood, he was unable to give vent to the joyful, if somewhat egotistical, sentiment which is recorded of him elsewhere. He sat in a corner, under the window, listening to the weird moaning of the night-wind without, now tapping at the door like a wayfarer, now whistling in the chimney like a sweep, now seeming to wander, darkly muttering, like some mysterious wild thing in the copse around the cottage, now rushing like some vast monster over the roof with a hoarse roar rising to a piping shriek as it died away. Then came violent rattling at the window above him, which grew louder and fiercer till Jack expected the glass to fly to pieces, and the next moment he fancied he could hear a hoarse voice, muffled by coming through the window say, "Let me in, why can't you let me in?" The vague, mystified awe that he had felt at the thousand suggestive voices of the wind changed into weird terror, and he cowered beneath the window striving not to look round, but compelled to turn by the horrible fascination of the presence of something behind him. He turned, threw open the window and looked out into the night. At first he could see nothing but the darkness, but the next moment he made out a broad, weird, goblin face with goggle eyes and a broad, queer hat, peering in through the window. "You're wanted," said the creature who appeared to be some species of watchman, in a muffled voice. "What for, Sir?" gasped Jack faintly. "You," said the goblin, "are commissioned by the local Board of Good Fairies to find the Mare's Nest. The Grey Mare, who built her nest in the suburbs of Creation, where people don't so much mind what they do, has a large family, all mares and all grey, except one, the youngest, who is as black as night, and as weird. And she is called the Nightmare. Her you must catch and tame and saddle and bridle, and she is the only steed you shall ever ride."

"And who are you, Sir?" asked the boy in some wonder.

"I am the Wind," answered the Spirit. "I fill the ears of men with a thousand voices, but never before have mortal eyes seen me. I go where I list and sing what song I please. I alone can guide you to the land of the Mare's Nest. Catch hold of my cloak."

A deep, solemn fear at his heart made Jack lay hold of the mantle obediently, the Wind turned with a whistle, and the next moment Jack was jerked bodily out of the window and carried away far over the house-tops under the midnight sky, hanging on behind to the vast, wild coat-tails of the guide. They left the city, with its roofs and chimney-pots, behind, and passed on over fields and lanes, over glens and ravines, on over dim, barren wildernesses. For hours they flew, leaving the bats and owls behind, till they came to a low, lonely wall, beside which there was a dilapidated notice board, looking the other way, stating that trespassers would be prosecuted, by order of somebody, no one quite knew who.

And beyond the wall there appeared to be nothing but mist and moonshine. And the Wind turned and said gravely, "Can't go any farther, Sir, not my beat. But that's your way." And jerking his head in the direction of the mysterious land over the wall, he moved away. And Jack clambered over the wall and entered the borderland of Creation. Before he had gone very far he came to a drop in the barren moors, which showed him the broad pale face of the moon, ten times as large as usual, and dark against it the lank melancholy figure of what looked like an overgrown calf. He came nearer, and had to violently pull the large animal's tail before he consented to take the least notice of his presence. Then he slowly swung round, a large, pale, overgrown head, with round rolling eyes, and looked abstractedly at the wayfarer. "Can you tell me, where is the Mare's Nest?" asked Jack.

The Calf eyed him wistfully for a moment, and then replied in a melancholy voice, with what appeared to be an impromptu rhyme of doubtful relevancy:

> "Oh, my limbs are very feeble,
>   My head is very big,
>   My ears are round, O do not, pray
>   Mistake me for a pig."

"Well, who wants to?" said the exasperated Horner. "I only want to be directed."

The Calf lifted his eyes to the moon a moment and then sang plaintively:

> "This Calf was the Mooncalf, the Cow was the Moon,
>   She died from effects of a popular tune,
>   And now in her glory she shines in the sky;
>   Oh, never had Calf such a mother as I."

And so sweet and pathetic for the moment was the upward look of the poor monster that Jack was quite touched and forgot his own

business and just stroked the lean ribs of the Mooncalf. And after
a long pause there rose again from the creature the wild queer songs
of worship:

"I forget all the creatures that taunt and despise,
When through the dark night-mists my mother doth rise,
She is tender and kind and she shines the night long
On her lunatic child as he sings her his song.
I was dropped on the dim earth to wander alone,
And save this pale monster no child she hath known.
Without like on the earth, without sister or brother,
I sit here and sing to my mystical mother."

And he sat there and sang for the remainder of the interview and
as Jack, slowly and almost reluctantly, made his way onward over the
dark moors, he could still hear the plaintive songs of the poetic
Mooncalf rising, a solitary hum upon that gloomy waste, to the white
moon overhead.

And he went on until he came to what appeared to be a low garden
wall, along which he ran until he came to where it sloped down a little
to a small wooden gate, and looking through he saw a strange spectacle.
The whole of the sloping downs beyond, as far almost as to the horizon,
were apparently cultivated like a gigantic kitchen garden, on which
grew enormous turnips, almost entirely above ground, with round
goblin eyes, that glimmered in ranks like gas-lamps lining all the slopes
under the night-sky. And above these armies of goblin turnips on the
hill was a little thatched cottage, apparently belonging to the Gardener.
Presently, as he stood there, staring at this singular back-garden, one
or two of the round, glowing eyes suddenly went out, and a dull,
gibbering moan came out of the darkness. The next moment the door
of the cottage opened and a tall, bony figure with a turned-down broad
hat and a demoniac-looking rake came out of the cottage and, rolling
round a pair of eyes as bright and glowing as theirs, requested to know
what was the matter.

"The light's gone out, oh, the light's gone out," moaned the turnips.
The Gardener retired into the house, and came out again with a short
candle burning in each hand. He made his way through the lines of
turnips. Opening a door in the back of their heads, he placed the light

inside, and instantly two pairs of eyes glared out as fiercely as ever. Back came the Gardener, taking half a mile at a stride over the wide downs of his kitchen-garden, and as he came back he saw Jack, who was peeping through the wooden paling.

"Who are you?" he roared with a voice like thunder.

"I am Jack Horner," replied that intrepid individual.

The nursery rhymes had not formed part of the Gardener's course of reading, so he knitted his brow and bellowed. "Do you know where you are?"

"Well, not altogether," replied the boy. "Where am I?"

"This," replied the tall Gardener, "is the garden of the turnip-ghosts. They are grown and sent to Covent Garden every morning. They have a great sale among people of your race, but none of your race ever came here before, or shall again. Come, you won't object to being buried up to the neck and having a candle put inside your head, will you?"

"Indeed, I shall object very much," replied Jack stoutly. "And what's more, I shan't do it."

"Shan't is rude," said the tall Gardener, showing a row of gleaming teeth, and, making a sudden dart, he lifted Jack by the collar and dropped him inside the enclosure. Jack, however, was not beaten so easily, but running full tilt at the Gardener he upset him with a bang among the turnips, sending his long rake flying ten miles off. But the Giant was on his feet again in a moment, and, snatching his largest flower-pot, he hurled it so as to come down neatly enclosing Jack underneath; but the boy kicked it to pieces and clutching the nearest missiles, two large turnips, which he tore up by the roots, he hurled them at the head of his enemy, who sent them back with additions. Then began a battle worthy of an epic. For days and nights they fought each other all over the hills, tearing up the turnips by thousands and flinging them pell-mell about the land. And at the end of a week's fighting, there was not a turnip lighted or growing in the land, but here and there a dying candle would make a dismal flame in the chaotic darkness. And the Gardener went aimlessly about the world, looking for his hat, and Jack continued his pilgrimage.

And at last he came to a strange land, where the rocks and mountain crests seemed as ragged and fantastic as the clouds of sunset, where wild and sudden lights, breaking out in nooks and clefts, were all that lit the sombre twilight of the world. And one day, as he wandered over the rocks and dales, he heard, suddenly, sounding through the darkness from over his head, a kind of long, shrill, demoniac neigh, which echoed weirdly over the lonely hills. And perched upon a hill-crest far above the dark mists, he could see the outline of what looked like a grey foal, looking down into the valley. The next moment the wild sound echoed again and it disappeared. Then he said to himself, "I am near the nest of the Grey Mare."

And after walking for a long time there came a fierce glare of light behind the hills, and he saw on the loftiest and most mysterious crest the fantastic head and mane of a great grey mare, perched in a nest like an eagle's. After a long climb he came to the base of the cliff on which the nest was perched and he could see the Grey Mare rolling her fiery eyes far over the lonely world; and scattered over the crags beneath her weird brood of mares were playing their demoniac gambols. And farthest of all, on the brink of an awful precipice, was the long black form and floating mane of the Nightmare, the darkest and most hideous of all. And when he saw it he gave a cry and ran towards it. All the grey mares, wandering like ghosts about the slopes, eyed him doubtfully as he went past, but the Nightmare, when she saw him, gave a scream like thunder and skipped wildly down the other side of the hill, whither Jack followed her. Then began a chase in which leagues and months were covered. Now the Nightmare would be flying far ahead of him, like a startled deer, far over the level plain and moors, now, with a still more maddening agility, she would be dancing indolently a few feet in front of him, in and out among the rocks, seeming to suggest by the very tossing of her long tail her contempt for human pursuit. Sometimes she would stand on her head a few yards off and smile at him till he came near, then flash off and grin at him round the corner of a rock. But neither his failure nor her scorn could make the stubborn little boy give up his appointed task, and in time he began to see the reward for his persistence.

The Nightmare began to lose her temper and try to get rid of him, thereby denoting that she no longer felt herself equal to the race, till at length, when they came to the strand of a moaning sea, close under a level face of cliffs, the Nightmare ran along at a quick trot till she came to a round hole in the rocks, which looked ten times too small for her, gave a squirm and vanished inside. Jack began to feel that things were even getting a little, as it were, unusual, if one may say so, but he clenched his hands and crept into the hole, which only just held him, and crawled along a dark low passage, at the end of which, upon a heap of skulls and bones, sat the Nightmare with gleaming eyes and teeth, and he knew that she was at bay. But Jack, who always felt compassion at inopportune moments, was willing to make an amicable arrangement. "Why do you object to my riding on you?" he asked. "I wish you no harm, but rather that we may both help each other. All things should help each other. It is the will of the Central Board."

"Mortal," replied the Nightmare, with a hideous laugh. "Dost though not know that I am no common mare. The Nightmare am I, the child of horror, and mine is it to ride upon thee. Many myriads of thy race have I ridden and made them my slaves, oppressing them with visions." And with that her eyes flamed terribly and her nose seemed to grow longer and longer as she came towards him. The next moment they were struggling for the mastery, rolling over one another, so that now one was uppermost and now the other.

And when Jack was undermost, with the black fiend sitting grinning on his chest, strange trances fell upon him and he fancied that he was falling from heights and fleeing down interminable roads, with a strange hopelessness in everything. And when, with a mighty effort, he cast them off, and threw his enemy under him, he found himself upon a silent moor under the starlight. So, through a long night, they kept changing places, till at last, after one fierce, foaming struggle— side by side, Jack rose uppermost, and tossed back his dishevelled hair, and the Nightmare sank helpless beneath him. She appeared to have fainted, and, after what the poor lady had gone through, it was perhaps not to be wondered at.

And Jack took the big, ugly head in his lap and kissed it and guarded it in silence, till at last the Nightmare opened her eyes, now as mild as the Mooncalf's, whinnied sorrowfully and rubbed her head against him. At last the Nightmare rose and stood silent and ready and Jack sprang upon her back and they rode away. And as they went, they passed by the Mooncalf, who was sitting on a stone, singing, with his tail feebly beating time.

> "On thy poor offspring thy pale beams be given,
> Turning the dull moor to white halls of heaven,
> And in my songs, O Cow, from your memory slide off
> The painful effects of the tune that you died of.
> We sit here alone, but a joy to each other,
> The light to the child and the songs to the mother."

He feared at first lest the grisly form of the Nightmare should frighten the poor Mooncalf, as indeed it frightened everything else on his way, but fears, like every other emotion save the filial, were unknown to the pale and lonely monstrosity. He was quite content, gazing plaintively up to the moon, and let the grim Nightmare go by as if it were the most conventional of quadrupeds. Once men had tried to domesticate the Mooncalf by taking it into the land of sunlight and decorating it with laurels, but it pined and wailed pathetically for the moon, which was proverbially absurd. And at last it broke loose from the everyday world and wandered away again into the land of moonshine, far more happy than many people would believe.

Meanwhile Jack and his dark steed had made their way to the wall and the notice-board, and re-entered the land of the real. But before he had gone far over the hard fields and stony ways of the old world, Jack saw that the poor Nightmare was limping and stumbling lamentably, and remembered that shoes were not provided in the vicinity of which she had been an inhabitant. Leading her with all speed to the nearest town he interviewed a blacksmith, who agreed to shoe her for the usual consideration. But the curious, not to say discommoding, part of the proceeding was that the Nightmare, who walked as mildly as a lamb while Jack himself was holding her, no sooner did the latter let go and the blacksmith approached her with a shoe than she gave a demoniac roar and kicked him through the roof. The apprentices and bystanders made a rush to secure the animal, but she fired out like a prize fighter; her legs appeared to have about twenty joints, from the way in which they flashed and curled about, knocking down man after man.

She appeared to thoroughly enjoy the fight, which was more than they did: her eyes glared with a lurid flame, her teeth and tongue protruded derisively, she appeared to grow more frightful every moment. None of the men dared approach her, as she sat viciously rubbing her nose with her hoof and grinning at them.

"Aha," she said, scornfully, "worms of mortal race, would ye lift your puny iron machinery against the living machinery of infernal life. Well may ye tremble, for my shadow is in your doors, and I will eat out your hearts with terror." Just at this promising stage of affairs, Jack came quietly forward with a hammer in one hand and the shoe in the other. The moment the flaring eyes of the monster encountered his face, she moaned and bowed her head, and Jack, taking the tools into his own hand, shoed her himself and rode away. And as he passed through the streets all the people murmured and hooted, and one man incautiously got in the way, whereupon the Nightmare spurned him over the chimney pots and the rest preserved a respectful distance.

Now it so happened that the King was resolved to hold a great display of tournaments in the town, to which came all the knights and warriors of his and the neighbouring countries. And when the lists were ready under the throne and bannered galleries and canopies, there rode forth on either side, with flaming crests and snorting chargers, the mightiest tilters of the land. And third of those who entered the lists, after the Prince Valentine of Vandala, and Lord Breacan of the Lance, rode a wild-eyed bare-headed boy, on a lank, black mare, broken-kneed, with a mane and tail brushing the ground. And all the while the broken-kneed mare and her rider stood silent. Suddenly, at the turning point of the fight, when Prince Valentine threw down his strongest opponent and rose victorious over the thick of the fray, the strange boy shook the hair from his forehead, levelled his rude spear and whispered something to his dismal and shabby steed. The mare gave a piercing yell that made the whole company jump out of their skin, and went like a thunderbolt, so that the boy's spear smote Prince Valentine on the vizor and laid him neatly on his back.

The Prince sprang up, amid the shouts, and flew at him, sword in hand, but ere either could strike, the Nightmare, who now stood as dismal as ever, showed its frightful teeth and, biting the weapon off short, munched it up with much apparent enjoyment. The Prince retired cursing, but Breacan of the Lance, a mailed giant, with a spear like a ship's mast, galloped down upon them. The Nightmare gave a hideous grin and, shooting forward, squirmed and vanished suddenly, rider and all, between the front legs of the giant's horse, so that in another moment he was suddenly shot head over heels and rolled on the ground.

The boy rode forward to the King's throne. "Give me the prize," he cried. "I and my good steed have vanquished the victors."

The King started to his feet, and his brow was dark. "There is some sorcery," he said, "in this boy and his black jade. Secure him."

The boy laughed. "Secure me yourself, liar," he said. "While I ride my mare, you may try." He was about to turn away, but the Nightmare took matters into her own hands. With a roar like a clap of thunder she shot forward, upset throne and King and the next moment was miles away on the moors. "Come," said the boy dismounting, "since men will not receive us, we will go on our way together. Perhaps we will visit the Mooncalf again and see your mother and your brothers."

"My master," said the Nightmare, sitting down at his feet. "I have no mother nor brothers. I know no one but you, who does not shrink from me. But you are my master and I will go with you whither you will."

PART TWO
From the Land of Nightmare

The Long Bow

Come, let us tell each other stories. There was once a king who was very fond of listening to stories, like the king in the Arabian Nights. The only difference was that, unlike that cynical Oriental, this king believed all the stories that he heard. It is hardly necessary to add that he lived in England. His face had not the swarthy secrecy of the tyrant of the thousand tales; on the contrary, his eyes were as big and innocent as two blue moons; and when his yellow beard turned totally white he seemed to be growing younger. Above him hung still his heavy sword and horn, to remind men that he had been a tall hunter and warrior in his time: indeed, with that rusted sword he had wrecked armies. But he was one of those who will never know the world, even when they conquer it. Besides his love of this old Chaucerian pastime of the telling of tales, he was, like many old English kings, specially interested in the art of the bow. He gathered round him great archers of the stature of Ulysses and Robin Hood, and to four of these he gave the whole government of his kingdom. They did not mind governing his kingdom; but they were sometimes a little bored with the necessity of telling him stories. None of their stories were true; but the king believed all of them, and this became very depressing. They created the most preposterous romances; and could not get the credit of creating them. Their true ambition was sent empty away. They were praised as archers; but they desired to be praised as poets. They were trusted as men, but they would rather have been admired as literary men.

At last, in an hour of desperation, they formed themselves into a club or conspiracy with the object of inventing some story which even the king could not swallow. They called it The League of the Long Bow; thus attaching themselves by a double bond to their motherland of England, which has been steadily celebrated since the Norman Conquest for its heroic archery and for the extraordinary credulity of its people.

At last it seemed to the four archers that their hour had come. The king commonly sat in a green curtained chamber, which opened by four doors, and was surmounted by four turrets. Summoning his champions to him on an April evening, he sent out each of them by a separate door, telling him to return at morning with the tale of his journey. Every champion bowed low, and, girding on great armour as for awful adventures, retired to some part of the garden to think of a lie. They did not want to think of a lie which would deceive the king; any lie would do that. They wanted to think of a lie so outrageous that it would not deceive him, and that was a serious matter.

The first archer who returned was a dark, quiet, clever fellow, very dexterous in small matters of mechanics. He was more interested in the science of the bow than in the sport of it. Also he would only shoot at a mark, for he thought it cruel to kill beasts and birds, and atrocious to kill men. When he left the king he had gone out into the wood and tried all sorts of tiresome experiments about the bending of branches and the impact of arrows; when even he found it tiresome he returned to the house of the four turrets and narrated his adventure. "Well," said the king, "what have you been shooting?" "Arrows," answered the archer. "So I suppose," said the king smiling; "but I mean, I mean what wild things have you shot?" "I have shot nothing but arrows," answered the bowman obstinately. "When I went out on to the plain I saw in a crescent the black army of the Tartars, the terrible archers whose bows are of bended steel, and their bolts as big as javelins. They spied me afar off, and the shower of their arrows shut out the sun and made a rattling roof above me. You know, I think it wrong to kill a bird, or worm, or even a Tartar. But such is the precision and rapidity of perfect science that, with my own arrows, I split every arrow as it came against me. I struck every flying shaft as if it were a flying bird. Therefore, Sire, I may say truly, that I shot nothing but arrows." The king said, "I know how clever you engineers are with your fingers." The archer said, "Oh," and went out.

The second archer, who had curly hair and was pale, poetical, and rather effeminate, had merely gone out into the garden and stared at the moon. When the moon had become too wide, blank, and watery, even for his own wide, blank, and watery eyes, he came in again. And when the king said "What have you been shooting?" he answered with great volubility, "I have shot a man; not a man from Tartary, not a man from Europe, Asia, Africa, or America; not a man on this earth at all. I have shot the Man in the Moon." "Shot the Man in the Moon?" repeated the king with something like a mild surprise. "It is easy to prove it," said the archer with hysterical haste. "Examine the moon through this particularly powerful telescope, and you will no longer find any traces of a man there." The king glued his big blue idiotic eye to the telescope for about ten minutes, and then said, "You are right: as you have often pointed out, scientific truth can only be tested by the senses. I believe you." And the second archer went out, and being of a more emotional temperament burst into tears.

The third archer was a savage, brooding sort of man with tangled hair and dreamy eyes, and he came in without any preface, saying, "I have lost all my arrows. They have turned into birds." Then as he saw that they all stared at him, he said, "Well, you know everything changes on the earth; mud turns into marigolds, eggs turn into chickens; one can even breed dogs into quite different shapes. Well, I shot my arrows at the awful eagles that clash their wings round the Himalayas; great gold eagles as big as elephants, which snap the tall trees by perching on them. My arrows fled so far over mountain and valley that they turned slowly into fowls in their flight. See here," and he threw down a dead bird and laid an arrow beside it. "Can't you see they are the same structure. The straight shaft is the backbone; the sharp point is the beak; the feather is the rudimentary plumage. It is merely modification and evolution." After a silence the king nodded gravely and said, "Yes; of course everything is evolution." At this the third archer suddenly and violently left the room, and was heard in some distant part of the building making extraordinary noises either of sorrow or of mirth.

The fourth archer was a stunted man with a face as dead as wood, but with wicked little eyes close together, and very much alive. His comrades dissuaded him from going in because they said that they had soared up into the seventh heaven of living lies, and that there was literally nothing which the old man would not believe. The face of the little archer became a little more wooden as he forced his way in, and when he was inside he looked round with blinking bewilderment. "Ha, the last," said the king heartily, "welcome back again!"

There was a long pause, and then the stunted archer said, "What do you mean by 'again'? I have never been here before." The king stared for a few seconds, and said, "I sent you out from this room with the four doors last night." After another pause the little man slowly shook his head. "I never saw you before," he said simply; "You never sent me out from anywhere. I only saw your four turrets in the distance, and strayed in here by accident. I was born in an island in the Greek Archipelago; I am by profession an auctioneer, and my name is Punk." The king sat on his throne for seven long instants like a statue; and then there awoke in his mild and ancient eyes an awful thing; the complete conviction of untruth. Every one has felt it who has found a child obstinately false. He rose to his height and took down the heavy sword above him, plucked it out naked, and then spoke. "I will believe your mad tales about the exact machinery of arrows; for that is science. I will believe your mad tales about traces of life in the moon; for that is science. I will believe your mad tales about jellyfish turning into gentlemen, and everything turning into anything; for that is science. But I will not believe you when you tell me what I know to be untrue. I will not believe you when you say that you did not all set forth under my authority and out of my house. The other three may conceivably have told the truth; but this last man has certainly lied. Therefore I will kill him." And with that the old and gentle king ran at the man with uplifted sword; but he was arrested by the roar of happy laughter, which told the world that there is, after all, something which an Englishman will not swallow.

The Three Dogs

Argus, the noble hound, that died at the feet of Odysseus, had long been a household word in Ithaca; and while (in the old Minoan phrase) there was life in the old dog yet, he would often give advice to the younger dogs that belonged to the Suitors and were, like their masters, puppies. He would tell them fables of the first days in the manner of a canine Aesop; and this is one of his tales.

Once upon a time there were Three Dogs, who hunted together

like a small pack. And it is said that, in the Golden Age, they never strove against each other, but had a treaty by which they took all things in turn; of which legendary time a memory remains in common speech, in the Ithican saying that every dog has his day. But one morning, as they went along the road in amity, they met Hermes, the god of trade, who desired it always to be free; and he mocked at this mildness they inherited from the age of the elder gods. He said that only by dogs fighting in rivalry could the best dog be developed, or the production of bones increased. So that the whole city became the scene of one furious and interminable dog-fight; the three dogs snatching bones from each other, until two of them were always hungry and the third horribly watchful; and all the town started at them in terror, for they were haggard and ferocious as wolves.

And about this time they met again with Hermes the god of the merchants (and, as some say, also of thieves) when he was out walking with great Plutus, the god of gold. And Hermes mocked at the emaciation he had made, and cried "There is hardly enough of them, all three, to make one good dog put together."

And Plutus, looking cunning, answered: 'And indeed, why not? For I have now in bondage Hephaestus of the Forge, that was the god of craftsmen; and he has still such cunning tricks as belong to a god that has become a slave. And in his enchanted furnace, I doubt not but it is possible to weld these three into one. We might make a creature that had three mouths with which to bark and awaken the town, and three sets of teeth with which to bite and terrify beggars and rioters; and yet have only one body to feed — to the general thrift."

Then was Hermes overjoyed and cried aloud: "This shall be the wonder of the ages, and do work never known before, for the good of gods and men."

So did the god of crafts labour and create the marvel: the dog that could work as three and feed as one; and the other gods bore it proudly up to heaven, where dwell the peacocks of Hera and the holy eagle of Zeus. Above them suddenly, like summer lightning in that dome of light, they heard the answer of the Father of Gods and Men: "He is indeed worthy, as you say, of some great work. Cleave then the rock down to the roots of the abyss and uncover the place of abominable things; for he is worthy to be the warden of Hell."

The Curious Englishman

The trees closed over us in a complete dome of foliage; but the sun was so strong that it glared through the translucent leaves as if through coloured glass of green and gold. We were sitting at one of those singular woodland restaurants which the Germans, with their instinct at once for the obvious and the picturesque, scatter along the line of their toy railways in their ornamental forests. To come upon such a place is like coming upon the house which Hansel and Gretel found in the German forest, the house made of things to eat. This house was also largely made of things to eat, and we began to eat it. My German friend spread on his plate a colour scheme of sausages, and procured a beer mug like a moderate-sized tower. I ordered a glass of white German wine, and took from my knapsack the remains of what had once been English biscuits, but were now in the last stage of dissolution. It was when we had finished this slight refreshment, and I was expecting either a rich conversation or a rich silence (in both of which all nice Germans excel), that the awful thing happened. It came like a thunderbolt. My companion shut down sharply the lid of his mug.

The waiters staggered back to right and left. For you must know that in Germany this is a signal that a man will drink no more. If he does not make the signal, but leaves the lid open, the attendants go on pouring in beer with the automatic placidity of a quiet river flowing over the stones. The intellectual principle of the thing is subtle and interesting. These waiters seem to regard drinking beer as the normal state of a human being. Not drinking beer they regard as a positive, exceptional, and even daring, action, to be emphasised by some startling signal. My friend made this startling signal, and almost immediately stood upright.

"You will come," he said earnestly, "and see the Roman camp; the Roman remains?"

"My friend," I replied equally earnestly, "I will not come and see the Roman camp; the Roman remains. I will stop where I am, and drink this Roman wine and eat these ancient Roman biscuits."

"They look ancient," he replied, "but scarcely Roman."

"What language is 'bis'," I asked, "and of what past participle is 'cuit' a corruption? Where did you learn the word 'wine'? and who planted vines in your valleys? You may go and look at ruins; for you think that the old civilization is dead. But I think the old civilization is still alive; and I will no more weep because this one Roman camp is in ruins, than I will weep because this one English biscuit is in ruins. In the same way you think Christianity is dead; so naturally you go and look at Christian abbeys. But I think Christianity is still alive, and I can go and look at Christian tram-cars. Rome and what it stands for is not for me a thing for museums. So I will sit on this ancient Roman stool at this ancient Roman table and eat my ancient Roman lunch. Roman camp! Why, all Europe is still a camp, and a Roman camp! Roman remains! Why, what are you and I but Roman remains? Let us look at each other."

"At any rate," said my friend, putting on his hat, "I am not a remains, for I am not remaining."

"I suppose I shall have to go with you," I said, getting to my feet, "and to enliven the unsupportable stupidity of sightseeing I will tell you a true story. I will tell you a little tale about a great man I once met, of whom it is sufficient to say that compared with him I am a sightseer."

I was once passing across Normandy in my boyhood, and seeing for the first time the tall, flamboyant churches which stand like tall, eternal lilies in that garden of architecture. I was a sightseer in those days, and a very good thing too. Now, in the long list of the splendid spired towns of which I wished to see as many as possible, there was one which was a doubtful case. It lay a long way out of the route, and was itself tiny and trivial, save for certain details about the parish church, which were said to join the Renaissance and the later Medieval building in a somewhat strange way. After some hesitation I left the main journey and took the long loop that led me to this minor curiosity. It was a small hill standing in the middle of an immense plain with poplars. The church hung on the crest of the hill, the town lay at the bottom, and it was as dull a town as there can well be in the world.

It was ugly with the extreme ugliness of French utilitarianism, and rigid to the very final pitch of French respectability. It was also very small, and seemed like a forgotten suburb of the universe. Leaving my baggage in a desolate café, I climbed the hill, and with considerable relief reached the church, the only place that could possibly repay the visit. And it did repay it. Without being so striking in general design as some of the great Norman churches, it had a quaint conglomeration of the two great styles, the late Christian and the revived Pagan, which could scarcely be seen so well elsewhere. There were actually caryatids in the confusion of Gothic ornament. It seemed like some great struggle in stone, and the war between the saints and the heathen heroes in a moment of its frenzy frozen for ever.

I descended the hill and re-entered that repulsive little town. I went into the dingy café and asked for dinner, and when I sat down to it I found to my supreme astonishment that there was another Englishman quietly eating his dinner opposite.

He was a man with a carefully pointed beard, hair touched with grey, and eyes touched with a sort of satire; he had very much the look of a certain kind of young Oxford don; I mean the tolerable kind. We fell into conversation first about the weather, then about the sky, then about heaven and hell, and everything there is. It is literally true that I have hardly ever in my life met a man with more real intellectual force. He knew things as they are known, not merely by a man who is learned, but by a man who is learning — that is, who is still alive. He talked like a man of the world, but also like a man of all the other worlds. In the course of some conversation (I think about Buddha), I asked him if he had arrived that afternoon.

"No," he replied carelessly, "I came here first four years ago."

"Great Heavens!" I cried, quite startled. "Have you been in this hole for four years? Have you never left it?"

"Yes," he said simply. "I once went out for a week. I found a railway train, and got into it. It brought me back here."

Then, as if dreamily, he added, "An omen, perhaps. I suppose I shall die here."

"Have you any reason for stopping here?" I asked.

"Not the faintest reason," he replied, with a sort of languid fervour. For a moment I was stunned to find such a man chained to such a spot. Then I suddenly remembered the church.

"After all," I said, "I suppose that architecture is inexhaustible. A good Gothic church is a sort of human forest. One could live in an old church and actually even find novelty. I suppose you have not got to the end of that church yet."

"I have not got to the beginning of it," he answered, calmly finishing his coffee. "I have never been up to look at it."

I never saw again the ugly town or the beautiful church or the incomprehensible man who clung to the ugly town and would not look at the beautiful church. I do not know whether he meant how little we should think of lovely things or how happy we can really be with dull things. But he meant something; he was that kind of man.

"If you ask me," said my German friend, "I should say that the police were looking for him." And with that we came out above the great curves of the Roman Camp.

A Nightmare

In the dimly lighted railway carriage a man had been talking to me about the structural weakness of St. Paul's Cathedral. He spoke in a bold, fresh, scientific spirit, and I suppose I had gone to sleep. At any rate, when I roused myself at Blackfriars Station and found myself alone I felt unusually chilly, and the station seemed unusually dark. I dropped on the dim platform, however, and went quickly across it, with the swinging rapidity of a routine, to the exit where stood the ticket-collector. He was not dressed like a ticket-collector, however. For some reason (possibly the cold I had myself remarked) he was cloaked from head to foot in a black hooded gown, such as had been worn centuries before by those friars after whom the place was named. And instead of taking my ticket he only said to me, "Do not go upstairs."

I looked at him with a dull wonder, and then I looked around equally doubtfully. It seemed to me that other monkish forms had gathered in the shadows, and that the place was like a monastery, with every light extinguished.

"Do not go upstairs," said the hooded man. "You will not like what is being done there. A man like you had far better stay with us."

"Do you calmly propose," I asked, "that I should stay in the Underground for ever?"

"Yes, in the Underground," he answered. "We of the ancient Church remained in the Underground, in the Catacombs. For what was done in the daylight was not good for a good man to see."

"What on earth is it?" I asked. "Is there a massacre?"

"Would to God," he answered, "that it were only that!"

"I will go up!" I cried. "It is open air, at any rate."

"Consider it well," he answered, with curious calm. "We guard ourselves with walls; we gird ourselves with sackcloth. But our laughter and our levity are within. But the new philosophers are girt all round with gaiety, and their despair is in their hearts."

"I will go up," I cried, and broke past him and ran upstairs.

Yet I did it with such swollen and expectant passions that I took it for granted that I should rush out upon some enormous orgy, obvious and obscene in the sunlight. And it was like the first crash into cold water when I found myself in an utterly empty street, turned almost white by the moon.

I strode up the street, turned two corners, and stood before St. Paul's Cathedral. It stood up quite cold and colossal in the empty night, like the lost temple of some empty planet. Only, when I had stared a little while, I saw the foolish figure of a young man standing straddling on the uppermost steps, as if he owned the Cathedral.

The instant I had started to mount the steps he waved at me wildly and cried, "Have you got a new design?"

And as I paused irresolute there popped like rabbits out of their holes, three pale men from between the pillars, peering at me.

The young man ran half-way down the steps, and I saw that he had long wandering auburn hair and an impudent smile, but his face was whiter than a corpse's.

"We have cleared the London streets," he explained, "of everyone who has not a design. These three gentlemen have all got new designs. That one," he added, lowering his voice and pointing at one man, who had a hairless head and huge ears, "That one is Pyffer himself."

"And who is Pyffer?" I asked, staring at the man, whose horrible ears seemed to grow larger as I stared.

"You know the great pessimist, surely," he asked anxiously. "But you must not speak to him. He never speaks. He sometimes — seems to begin to speak, but it always ends in a yawn. Yet how well that yawn seems to express his terrible creed!"

I had reached the top step, and now saw the other two men more clearly: one was a blonde German with watery eyes and wild moustaches. The other was an elderly man with black whiskers and green spectacles. He was in the middle of an oration when I reached him.

"It is merely," he said, "a matter of science — a matter for experts. What could be more absurd than the present construction of the thing?"

At this point the pale young man (who seemed to be a sort of showman) whispered in my ear: "Dr. Blood; he has made Conduct a science."

Dr. Blood continued: "What can be more absurd, architecturally, than that singular object at the top of the cathedral; I mean the object with the projecting arms? Think of putting up a thing with projecting arms, and expecting it to stand upright? The ball, too, is obviously top-heavy. The dome is a curve. I am against curves."

He paused for an instant, and Professor Pyffer opened his mouth as if to speak. Then he opened his mouth as if to shout; and then he shut it in silence. He had only yawned.

"In that yawn," whispered the young man to me, "he has swallowed all the stars."

I replied that they did not seem to agree with him; but Dr. Blood was still going on.

"The matter is to an expert, obvious. The thing at the top should be a small cube of stone. The ball should be a cube of stone slightly larger. The dome should be represented by a cube larger still, and so on. If it were built like that, it would never fall down."

"Has it ever occurred to you," I asked, "that if it were built like that we should want it to fall down?"

"The stranger speaks right," broke in the fair man with the watery eyes. "It should be upwards ever! From the man to the superman! From the structure to the superstructure! I will tell you the fault of your architecture; it is not upon the nature-energy based! Your churches are larger at the bottom, smaller at the top. But the all-mother-born trees are smaller at the bottom, larger at the top. So should this cathedral be. In the first floor two domes, in the second floor three domes, in the third floor, and so on, ever branching, ever increasing, each landing larger than the last one, till at last…"

He had flung up his arms in a rigid ecstasy. His voice failed, but his arms remained vertical; so we all murmured "Quite so."

Then Dr. Blood said in a curious, cool voice, "Now you trust the expert. I'll put this place right in two minutes."

He strode into the interior, and then we heard three taps. And the next moment this dome that filled the sky shook as in an earthquake, and tilted sideways. Nothing could express the enormous unreason of that familiar scene silently gone wrong.

I awoke to hear the hoarse voice of the yawning man, speaking for the first and last time in my ear.

"Do you see," he whispered, "the sky is crooked?"

The Giant

When Jack the Giant Killer really first saw the giant his experience was not such as has been generally supposed. If you care to hear it I will tell you the real story of Jack the Giant Killer. To begin with, the most awful thing which Jack first felt about the giant was that he was not a giant. He came striding across an interminable wooded plain, and against its remote horizon the giant was quite a small figure, like a figure in a picture — he seemed merely a man walking across the grass. Then Jack was shocked by remembering that the grass which the man was treading down was one of the tallest forests upon that plain. The man came nearer and nearer, growing bigger and bigger, and at the instant when he passed the possible stature of humanity Jack almost screamed. The rest was an intolerable apocalypse.

The giant had the one frightful quality of a miracle: the more he became incredible the more he became solid. The less one could believe in him the more plainly one could see him. It was unbearable that so much of the sky should be occupied by one human face. His eyes which had stood out like bow windows, became bigger yet, and there was no metaphor that could contain their bigness; yet still they were human eyes. Jack's intellect was utterly gone under that huge hypnotism of the face that filled the sky; his last hope was submerged, his five wits all still with terror.

But there stood up in him still a kind of cold chivalry, a dignity of dead honour that would not forget the small and futile sword in his hand. He rushed at one of the colossal feet of this human tower, and when he came quite close to it the ankle-bone arched over him like a cave. Then he planted the point of his sword against the foot and leant on it with all his weight, till it went up to the hilt and broke the hilt, and then snapped just under it. And it was plain that the giant felt a sort of prick, for he snatched up his great foot into his great hand for an instant; and then, putting it down again, he bent over and stared at the ground until he had seen his enemy.

Then he picked up Jack between a big finger and thumb and threw him away; and as Jack went through the air he felt as if he were flying from system to system through the universe of stars. But, as the giant had thrown him away carelessly, he did not strike a stone, but struck soft mire by the side of a distant river. There he lay insensible for several hours; but when he awoke again his horrible conqueror was still in sight. He was striding away across the void and wooded plain towards where it ended in the sea; and by this time he was only much higher than any of the hills. He grew less and less indeed; but only as a really high mountain grows at last less and less when we leave it in a railway train. Half an hour afterwards he was a bright blue colour, as are the distant hills; but his outline was still human and still gigantic. Then the big blue figure seemed to come to the brink of the big blue sea, and even as it did so it altered its attitude. Jack, stunned and bleeding, lifted himself laboriously upon one elbow to stare. The giant once more caught hold of his ankle, wavered twice as in a wind, and then went over into the great sea which washes the whole world, and which, alone of all things God has made, was big enough to drown him.

The Tree of Pride

If you go down to the Barbary Coast, where the last wedge of the forest narrows down between the desert and the great tideless sea, you will find the natives still telling a strange story about a saint of the Dark Ages. There, on the twilight border of the Dark Continent, you feel the Dark Ages. I have only visited the place once, though it lies so to speak, opposite to the Italian city where I lived for years, and yet you would hardly believe how the topsy-turveydom and transmigration of this myth somehow seemed less mad than they really are, with the wood loud with lions at night and that dark red solitude beyond. They say that the hermit St. Securis, living there among trees, grew to love them like companions; since, though great giants with many arms like Briareus, they were the mildest and most blameless of the creatures; they did not devour like the lions, but rather opened their arms to all the little birds. And he prayed that they might be loosened from time to time to walk like other things. And the trees were moved upon the prayers of Securis, as they were at the songs of Orpheus. The men of the desert were stricken from afar with fear, seeing the saint walking with a walking grove, like a schoolmaster with his boys. For the trees were thus freed under strict conditions of discipline. They were to return at the sound of the hermit's bell, and, above all, to copy the wild beasts in walking only — to destroy and devour nothing. Well, it is said that one of the trees heard a voice that was not the saint's; that, in the warm green twilight of one summer evening it became conscious of something sitting and speaking in its branches in the guise of a great bird, and it was that which once spoke from a tree in the guise of a great serpent. As the voice grew louder among its murmuring leaves the tree was torn with a great desire to stretch out and snatch at the birds that flew harmlessly about their nests, and pluck them to pieces. Finally, the tempter filled the tree-top with his own birds of pride, the starry pageant of the peacocks. And the spirit of the brute overcame the spirit of the tree, and it rent and consumed the blue-green birds till not a plume was left, and returned to the quiet tribe of trees. But they say that when spring came all the other trees put forth leaves, but this put forth feathers of a strange hue and pattern. And by that monstrous assimilation the saint knew of the sin, and he rooted that one tree to the earth with a judgement so that evil should fall on any who removed it again.

A Legend of Saint Francis

St. Francis, playing in the fields of heaven, had been informed by his spritual great-grandson Friar Bacon (who takes an interest in new and curious things) that the modern world was just about to witness a great celebration in honour of the great founder. St. Francis, out of his great love for his fellows, felt an ardent desire to be present; but the Blessed Thomas More, who had seen the modern world begin and had his doubts, shook his head with the melancholy humour that made him so charming a companion. "I fear," he said, "that you will find the present state of the world very distressing to your hopes of Holy Poverty and charity to all. Even when I left (rather abruptly) men were beginning to grab land greedily, to pile up gold and silver, to live for nothing but pleasure and luxury in the arts." St. Francis said he was prepared for that; but although he came down to the world in that sense prepared, as he walked about the world he was puzzled.

At first he had a kind of hope, not unmixed with holy fear, that all the people had become Franciscans. Nearly all of them were without land. Large numbers of them were without homes. If they had really all of them been grabbing property, it seems strange that hardly any of them had got any. Then he met a Philanthropist, who professed to have ideals very similar to his own, though less clearly expressed; and St. Francis had occasion to apologise, with all his characteristic good manners, for the fact that his vow forbade him to carry any gold or silver in his purse. "I never carry money about myself," said the Philanthropist nodding; "Our system of credit has become so complete that coins seem quite antiquated." Then he took out a little piece of paper and wrote on it; and the saint could not but admire the beautiful faith and simplicity with which this scribble was received as a substitute for cash. But when he went a little deeper into conversation with the Philanthropist, he grew more and more doubtful and troubled in his mind. For instance, it was doubtless in consequence of some highly respectable Vow that the Philanthropist and most other commercial persons were dressed in black and grey and other sober colours. Indeed they seemed, in a rapture of Christian humility, to have made themselves as hideous as possible; the shapes of their hats and trousers being quite horrible to the artistic sensibilities of the Italian. But when he began to talk with gentle awe about their sacrifice, and how hard he had himself felt it even to surrender the crimson cloaks and capes, the gilded belts and swordhilts of his own gay and gallant youth, he was mystified to find that the merchants of his own guild in this epoch had never felt even the obvious temptation to wear swords. More and more did he feel convinced that they were of a finer spiritual order than himself; but, as this was no new feeling for him, he continued to confide in these ascetics about the defects of his own asceticism. He told them how he had cried: "I may yet have children," and how much family life attracted him; at which they all laughed, and began to explain that few of them had any children or wanted any. And as they went on talking, that understanding which is terribly alert even in the most innocent of saints, began to creep upon him like a dreadful paralysis. It is uncertain whether he fully understood why and how they denied themselves this natural pleasure; but it is certain that he went rather hurriedly back to heaven. Nobody knows what saints really think; but he was said by some to have concluded that the bad men of his time were better than the good men of ours.

The Angry Street

I cannot remember whether this tale is true or not. If I read it through very carefully I have a suspicion that I should come to the conclusion that it is not. But, unfortunately, I cannot read it through very carefully, because, you see, it is not written yet. The image and idea of it clung to me through a great part of my boyhood; I may have dreamt it before I could talk; or told it to myself before I could read; or read it before I could remember. On the whole, however, I am certain that I did not read it. For children have very clear memories about things like that; and of the books of which I was really fond I can still remember not only the shape and bulk and binding, but even the position of the printed words on many of the pages. On the whole, I incline to the opinion that it happened to me before I was born.

*   *   *

At any rate, let us tell the story now with all the advantages of the atmosphere that has clung to it. You may suppose me, for the sake of argument, sitting at lunch in one of those quick-lunch restaurants in the City where men take their food so fast that it has none of the quality of food, and take their half-hour's vacation so fast that it has none of the qualities of leisure. To hurry through one's leisure is the most unbusiness-like of actions. They all wore tall shiny hats as if they could not lose an instant even to hang them on a peg, and they all had one eye a little off, hypnotized by the huge eye of the clock. In short they were the slaves of the modern bondage, you could hear their fetters clanking. Each was, in fact, bound by a chain; the heaviest chain ever tied to a man — it is called a watch-chain.

Now, among these there entered and sat down opposite to me a man who almost immediately opened an uninterrupted monologue. He was like all the other men in dress, yet he was startlingly opposite to them all in manner. He wore a high shiny hat and a long frock coat, but he wore them as such solemn things were meant to be worn; he wore the silk hat as if it were a mitre, and the frock coat as if it were the ephod of a high priest. He not only hung his hat up on the peg,

61

but he seemed (such was his stateliness) almost to ask permission of the hat for doing so, and to apologize to the peg for making use of it. When he had sat down on a wooden chair with the air of one considering its feelings and given a sort of slight stoop or bow to the wooden table itself, as if it were an altar, I could not help some comment springing to my lips. For the man was a big, sanguine-faced, prosperous-looking man, and yet he treated everything with a care that almost amounted to nervousness.

For the sake of saying something to express my interest I said, "This furniture is fairly solid; but, of course, people do treat it much too carelessly."

As I looked up doubtfully my eye caught his, and was fixed as his was fixed, in an apocalyptic stare. I had thought him ordinary as he entered, save for his strange, cautious manner; but if the other people had seen him then they would have screamed and emptied the room. They did not see him, and they went on making a clatter with their forks, and a murmur with their conversation. But the man's face was the face of a maniac.

"Did you mean anything particular by that remark?" he asked at last, and the blood crawled back slowly into his face.

"Nothing whatever," I answered. "One does not mean anything here; it spoils people's digestions."

He leaned back and wiped his broad forehead with a high handkerchief; and yet there seemed to be a sort of regret in his relief.

"I thought perhaps," he said in a low voice, "that another of them had gone wrong."

"If you mean another digestion gone wrong," I said, "I never heard of one here that went right. This is the heart of the Empire, and the other organs are in an equally bad way."

"No, I mean another street gone wrong," he said heavily and quietly, "but as I suppose that doesn't explain much to you, I think I shall have to tell you the story. I do so with all the less responsibility; because I know you won't believe it. For forty years of my life I invariably left my office, which is in Leadenhall Street, at half-past five in the afternoon, taking with me an umbrella in the right hand and a bag in the left hand. For forty years two months and four days I passed out of the side office door, walked down the street on the left-hand side, took the first turning to the left and the third to the right, from where I bought an evening paper, followed the road on the right-hand side round two obtuse angles, and came out just outside a Metropolitan station, where I took a train home. For forty years two months and four days I fulfilled this course by accumulated habit: it was not a long street that I traversed, and it took me about four and a half minutes to do it. After forty years two months and four days, on the fifth day I went out in the same manner, with my umbrella in the right hand and my bag in the left, and I began to notice that walking along the familiar street tired me somewhat more than usual. At first I thought I must be breathless and out of condition; though this, again, seemed unnatural, as my habits had always been like clockwork. But after a little while I became convinced that the road was distinctly on a more steep incline that I had known previously; I was positively panting uphill. Owing to this no doubt the corner of the street seemed further off than usual; and when I turned it I was convinced that I had turned down the wrong one. For now the street shot up quite a steep slant, such as one only sees in the hilly parts of London, and in this part there were no hills at all. Yet it was not the wrong street. The name written on it was the same; the shuttered shops were the same; the lamp-posts and the whole look of the perspective was the same; only it was tilted upwards like a lid. Forgetting any trouble about breathlessness or fatigue I ran furiously forward, and reached the second of my accustomed turnings, which ought to bring me almost within sight of the station. And as I turned that corner I nearly fell on the pavement. For now the street went up straight in front of my face like a steep staircase or the side of a pyramid. There was not for miles round that place so much as a slope like that of Ludgate Hill. And this was a slope like that of the Matterhorn. The whole street had lifted itself like a single wave, and yet every speck and detail of it was the same, and I saw in the high distance, as at the top of an Alpine pass, picked out in pink letters the name over my paper shop.

"I ran on and on blindly now, passing all the shops, and coming to a part of the road where there was a long grey row of private houses. I had, I know not why, an irrational feeling that I was on a long iron bridge in empty space. An impulse seized me, and I pulled up the iron trap of a coal hole. Looking down through it I saw empty space and the stars.

"When I looked up again a man was standing in his front garden, having apparently come out of his house; he was leaning over the railings and gazing at me. We were all alone on that nightmare road; his face was in shadow; his dress was dark and ordinary; but when I saw him standing so perfectly still I knew somehow that he was not of this world. And the stars behind his head were larger and fiercer than ought to be endured by the eyes of men.

" 'If you are a kind angel,' I said, 'or a wise devil, or have anything in common with mankind, tell me what is this street possessed of devils.'

"After a long silence he said, 'What do you say that it is?'

" 'It is Bumpton Street, of course,' I snapped. 'It goes to Oldgate Station.'

" 'Yes,' he admitted gravely; 'it goes there sometimes. Just now, however, it is going to heaven.'

" 'To heaven?' I said. 'Why?'

" 'It is going to heaven for justice,' he replied. 'You must have treated it badly. Remember always that there is one thing that cannot be endured by anybody or anything. That one unendurable thing is to be overworked and also neglected. For instance, you can overwork women — everybody does. But you can't neglect women — I defy you to. At the same time, you can neglect tramps and gipsies and all the apparent refuse of the State, so long as you do not overwork them. But no beast of the field, no horse, no dog can endure long to be asked to do more than his work and yet have less than his honour. It is the same with streets. You have worked this street to death, and yet you have never remembered its existence. If you had owned a healthy democracy, even of pagans, they would have hung this street with garlands and given it the name of a god. Then it would have gone quietly. But at last the street has grown tired of your tireless insolence; and it is bucking and rearing its head to heaven. Have you never sat on a bucking horse?'

"I looked at the long grey street, and for a moment it seemed to me to be exactly like the long grey neck of a horse flung up to heaven. But in a moment my sanity returned, and I said, 'But this is all nonsense. Streets go to the place they have to go to. A street must always go to its end.'

" 'Why do you think so of a street?' he asked, standing very still.

" 'Because I have always seen it do the same thing,' I replied, in reasonable anger. 'Day after day, year after year, it has always gone to Oldgate Station; day after...'

"I stopped, for he had flung up his head with the fury of the road in revolt.

" 'And you?' he cried terribly. 'What do you think the road thinks of you? Does the road think you are alive? Are you alive! Day after day, year after year, *you* have gone to Oldgate Station...' Since then I have respected the things called inanimate."

And bowing slightly to the mustard-pot, the man in the restaurant withdrew.

The Legend Of The Sword

A strange story is told of the Spanish-American War, of a sort that sounds like the echo of some elder epic: of how an active Yankee, pursuing the enemy, came at last to a forgotten Spanish station on an island and felt as if he had intruded on the presence of a ghost. For he found in a house hung with ragged Cordova leather and old gold tapestries, a Spaniard as out of time as Don Quixote, who had no weapon but an ancient sword. This he declared his family had kept bright and sharp since the days of Cortes: and it may be imagined with what a smile the American regarded it, standing spick and span with his Sam Browne belt and his new service revolver.

His amusement was naturally increased when he found, moored close by, the gilded skeleton of an old galley. When the Spanish spectre sprang on board, brandishing his useless weapon, and his captor followed, the whole parted amidships and the two were left clinging to a spar. And here (says the legend) the story took a strange turn: for they floated far on this rude raft together: and were ultimately cast up on a desert island.

The shelving shores of the island were covered with a jungle of rush and tall grasses; which it was necessary to clear away, both to make space for a hut and to plait mats or curtains for it. With an activity rather surprising in one so slow and old-fashioned, the Spaniard drew his sword and began to use it in the manner of a scythe. The other asked if he could assist.

"This, as you say, is a rude and antiquated tool," replied the swordsman, "and your own is a weapon of precision and promptitude. If, therefore, you (with your unerring aim) will condescend to shoot off each blade of grass, one at a time, who can doubt that the task will be more rapidly accomplished?"

The face of the Iberian, under the closest scrutiny, seemed full of gravity and even gloom: and the work continued in silence. In spite of his earthly toils, however, the Hidalgo contrived to remain reasonably neat and spruce: and the puzzle was partially solved one morning when the American, rising early, found his comrade shaving himself with the sword, which that foolish family legend had kept particularly keen.

"A man with no earthly possessions but an old iron blade," said the Spaniard apologetically, "must shave himself as best he can. But you, equipped as you are with every luxury of science, will have no difficulty in shooting off your whiskers with a pistol."

So far from profiting by this graceful felicitation, the modern traveller seemed for a moment a little ruffled or put out: then he said abruptly, unslinging his revolver, "Well, I guess I can't eat my whiskers, anyhow; and this little toy may be more use in getting breakfast."

And blazing away rapidly and with admirable aim, he brought down five birds and emptied his revolver.

"Let me assure you," said the other courteously, "that you have provided the materials for more than one elegant repast. Only after that, your ammunition being now exhausted, shall we have to fall back on a clumsy trick of mine, of spiking fish on the sword."

"You can spike me now, I suppose, as well as the fish," said the other bitterly. "We seem to have sunk back into a state of barbarism."

"We have sunk into a state," said the Spaniard, nodding gravely, "in which we can get anything we want with what we have got already."

"But," cried the American, "that is the end of all Progress!"

"I wonder whether it matters much which end?" said the other.

How I Found The Superman

Readers of Mr. Bernard Shaw and other modern writers may be interested to know that the Superman has been found. I found him; he lives in South Croydon. My success will be a great blow to Mr. Shaw, who has been following quite a false scent, and is now looking for the creature in Blackpool; and as for Mr. Wells's notion of generating him out of gases in a private laboratory, I always thought it doomed to failure. I assure Mr. Wells that the Superman at Croydon was born in the ordinary way, though he himself, of course, is anything but ordinary.

Nor are his parents unworthy of the wonderful being whom they have given to the world. The name of Lady Hypatia Smythe-Browne (now Lady Hypatia Hagg) will never be forgotten in the East End, where she did such splendid social work. Her constant cry of "Save the children!" referred to the cruel neglect of children's eyesight involved in allowing them to play with crudely painted toys. She quoted unanswerable statistics to prove that children allowed to look at violet and vermilion often suffered from failing eyesight in their extreme old age; and it was owing to her ceaseless crusade that the pestilence of the Monkey-on-the-Stick was almost swept from Hoxton. The devoted worker would tramp the streets untiringly, taking away the toys from all the poor children, who were often moved to tears by her kindness. Her good work was interrupted, partly by a new interest in the creed of Zoroaster, and partly by a savage blow from an umbrella. It was inflicted by a dissolute Irish apple-woman, who, on returning from some orgy to her ill-kept apartment, found Lady Hypatia in the bedroom taking down an oleograph, which, to say the least of it, could not really elevate the mind. At this the ignorant and partly intoxicated Celt dealt the social reformer a severe blow, adding to it an absurd accusation of theft. The lady's exquisitely balanced mind received a shock, and it was during a short mental illness that she married Dr. Hagg.

Of Dr. Hagg himself I hope there is no need to speak. Any one even slightly acquainted with those daring experiments in Neo-Individualist

Eugenics, which are now the one absorbing interest of the English democracy, must know his name and often commend it to the personal protection of an impersonal power. Early in life he brought to bear that ruthless insight into the history of religions which he had gained in boyhood as an electrical engineer. Later he became one of our greatest geologists; and achieved that bold and bright outlook upon the future of Socialism which only geology can give. At first there seemed something like a rift, a faint, but perceptible, fissure, between his views and those of his aristocratic wife. For she was in favour (to use her own powerful epigram) of protecting the poor against themselves; while he declared pitilessly, in a new and striking metaphor, that the weakest must go to the wall. Eventually, however, the married pair perceived an essential union in the unmistakably modern character of both their views; and in this enlightening and intelligible formula their souls found peace. The result is that this union of the two highest types of our civilization, the fashionable lady and the all but vulgar medical man, has been blessed by the birth of the Superman, that being whom all the labourers in Battersea are so eagerly expecting night and day.

*   *   *

I found the house of Dr. and Lady Hypatia Hagg without much difficulty; it is situated in one of the last straggling streets of Croydon, and overlooked by a line of poplars. I reached the door towards the twilight, and it was natural that I should fancifully see something dark and monstrous in the dim bulk of that house which contained the creature who was more marvellous than the children of men. When I entered the house I was received with exquisite courtesy by Lady Hypatia and her husband; but I found much greater difficulty in actually seeing the Superman, who is now about fifteen years old, and is kept by himself in a quiet room. Even my conversation with the father and mother did not quite clear up the character of this mysterious being. Lady Hypatia, who has a pale and poignant face, and is clad in those impalpable and pathetic greys and greens with which she has brightened so many homes in Hoxton, did not appear to talk of her offspring with any of the vulgar vanity of an ordinary human mother. I took a bold step and asked if the Superman was nice looking.

"He creates his own standard, you see," she replied, with a slight sigh. "Upon that plane he is more than Apollo. Seen from our lower plane, of course — " And she sighed again.

I had a horrible impulse, and said suddenly, "Has he got any hair?"

There was a long and painful silence, and then Dr. Hagg said smoothly: "Everything upon that plane is different; what he has got is not ... well, not, of course, what we call hair ... but — "

"Don't you think," said his wife, very softly, "don't you think that really, for the sake of argument, when talking to the mere public, one might call it hair?"

"Perhaps you are right," said the doctor after a few moments' reflection. "In connexion with hair like that one must speak in parables."

"Well, what on earth is it," I asked in some irritation, "if it isn't hair? Is it feathers?"

"Not feathers, as we understand feathers," answered Hagg in an awful voice.

I got up in some irritation. "Can I see him, at any rate?" I asked. "I am a journalist, and have no earthly motives except curiosity and personal vanity. I should like to say that I had shaken hands with the Superman."

The husband and wife had both got heavily to their feet, and stood, embarrassed.

"Well, of course, you know," said Lady Hypatia, with the really charming smile of the aristocratic hostess. "You know he can't exactly shake hands ... not hands, you know ... The structure, of course — "

I broke out of all social bounds, and rushed at the door of the room which I thought to contain the incredible creature. I burst it open; the room was pitch dark. But from in front of me came a small sad yelp, and from behind me a double shriek.

"You have done it, now!" cried Dr. Hagg, burying his bald brow in his hands. "You have let in a draught on him; and he is dead."

As I walked away from Croydon that night I saw men in black carrying out a coffin that was not of any human shape. The wind wailed above me, whirling the poplars, so that they drooped and nodded like the plumes of some cosmic funeral. "It is, indeed," said Dr. Hagg, "the whole universe weeping over the frustration of its most magnificent birth." But I thought that there was a hoot of laughter in the high wail of the wind.

Dukes

The Duc de Chambertin-Pommard was a small but lively relic of a really aristocratic family, the members of which were nearly all Atheists up to the time of the French Revolution, but since that event (beneficial in such various ways) had been very devout. He was a Royalist, a Nationalist, and a perfectly sincere patriot in that particular style which consists of ceaselessly asserting that one's country is not so much in danger as already destroyed. He wrote cheery little articles for the Royalist Press entitled "The End of France" or "The Last Cry," or what not, and he gave the final touches to a picture of the Kaiser riding across a pavement of prostrate Parisians with a glow of patriotic exultation. He was quite poor, and even his relations had no money. He walked briskly to all his meals at a little open café, and he looked just like everybody else.

Living in a country where aristocracy does not exist, he had a high opinion of it. He would yearn for the swords and the stately manners of the Pommards before the Revolution — most of whom had been (in theory) Republicans. But he turned with a more practical eagerness to the one country in Europe where the tricolour has never flown and men have never been roughly equalized before the State. The beacon and comfort of his life was England, which all Europe sees clearly as the one pure aristocracy that remains. He had, moreover, a mild taste for sport and kept an English bulldog, and he believed the English to be a race of bulldogs, of heroic squires, and hearty yeomen vassals, because he read all this in English Conservative papers, written by exhausted little Levantine clerks. But his reading was naturally for the most part in the French Conservative papers (though he knew English well), and it was in these that he first heard of the horrible Budget. There he read of the confiscatory revolution planned by the Lord Chancellor of the Exchequer, the sinister Georges Lloyd. He also read how chivalrously Prince Arthur Balfour of Burleigh had defied that demagogue, assisted by Austen, the Lord Chamberlain and the gay and witty Walter Lang. And being a brisk partisan and a capable journalist, he decided to pay England a special visit and report to his paper upon the struggle.

He drove for an eternity in an open fly through beautiful woods, with a letter of introduction in his pocket to one duke, who was to introduce him to another duke. The endless and numberless avenues of bewildering pine woods gave him a queer feeling that he was driving through the countless corridors of a dream. Yet the vast silence and freshness healed his irritation at modern ugliness and unrest. It seemed a background fit for the return of chivalry. In such a forest a king and all his court might lose themselves hunting or a knight errant might perish with no companion but God. The castle itself when he reached it was somewhat smaller than he had expected, but he was delighted with its romantic and castellated outline. He was just about to alight when somebody opened two enormous gates at the side and the vehicle drove briskly through.

"That is not the house?" he inquired politely of the driver.

"No, sir," said the driver, controlling the corners of his mouth. "The lodge, sir."

"Indeed," said the Duc de Chambertin-Pommard, "that is where the Duke's land begins?"

"Oh no, sir," said the man, quite in distress. "We've been in his Grace's land all day."

The Frenchman thanked him and leant back in the carriage, feeling as if everything were incredibly huge and vast, like Gulliver in the country of the Brobdingnags.

He got out in front of a long facade of a somewhat severe building, and a little careless man in a shooting jacket and knickerbockers ran down the steps. He had a weak, fair moustache and dull, blue, babyish eyes; his features were insignificant, but his manner extremely pleasant and hospitable. This was the Duke of Aylesbury, perhaps the largest landowner in Europe, and known only as a horsebreeder until he began to write abrupt little letters about the Budget. He led the French Duke upstairs, talking trivialities in a hearty way, and there presented him to another and more important English oligarch, who got up from a writing-desk with a slightly senile jerk. He had a gleaming bald head and glasses; the lower part of his face was masked with a short, dark beard, which did not conceal a beaming smile, not unmixed with sharpness. He stooped a little as he ran, like some sedentary head clerk or cashier; and even without the cheque-book and papers on his desk would have given the impression of a merchant or man of business. He was dressed in a light grey check jacket. He was the Duke of Windsor, the great Unionist statesman. Between these two loose, amiable men, the little Gaul stood erect in his black frock coat, with the monstrous gravity of French ceremonial good manners. This stiffness led the Duke of Windsor to put him at his ease (like a tenant), and he said, rubbing his hands:

"I was delighted with your letter... delighted. I shall be very pleased if I can give you — er — any details."

"My visit," said the Frenchman, "scarcely suffices for the scientific exhaustion of detail. I seek only the idea. The idea, that is always the immediate thing."

"Quite so," said the other rapidly; "quite so... the idea."

Feeling somehow that it was his turn (the English Duke having done all that could be required of him) Pommard had to say: "I mean the idea of aristocracy. I regard this as the last great battle for the idea. Aristocracy, like any other thing, must justify itself to mankind. Aristocracy is good because it preserves a picture of human dignity in a world where that dignity is often obscured by servile necessities. Aristocracy alone can keep a certain high reticence of soul and body, a certain noble distance between the sexes."

The Duke of Aylesbury, who had a clouded recollection of having squirted soda-water down the neck of a Countess on the previous evening, looked somewhat gloomy, as if lamenting the theoretic spirit of the Latin race. The elder Duke laughed heartily, and said: "Well, well, you know; we English are horribly practical. With us the great question is the land. Out here in the country... do you know this part?"

"Yes, yes," cried the Frenchman eagerly. "I see what you mean. The country! The old rustic life of humanity! A holy war upon the bloated and filthy towns. What right have these anarchists to attack your busy and prosperous countrysides? Have they not thriven under your management? Are not the English villages always growing larger and gayer under the enthusiastic leadership of their encouraging squires? Have you not the Maypole? Have you not Merry England?''

The Duke of Aylesbury made a noise in his throat, and then said very indistinctly: "They all go to London."

"All go to London?" repeated Pommard, with a blank stare. "Why?"

This time nobody answered, and Pommard had to attack again.

"The spirit of aristocracy is essentially opposed to the greed of the industrial cities. Yet in France there are actually one or two nobles so vile as to drive coal and gas trades, and drive them hard."

The Duke of Windsor looked at the carpet.

The Duke of Aylesbury went and looked out of the window. At length the latter said: "That's rather stiff, you know. One has to look after one's own business in town, as well."

"Do not say it," cried the little Frenchman, starting up. "I tell you all Europe is one fight between business and honour. If we do not fight for honour, who will? What other right have we poor two-legged sinners to titles and quartered shields except that we stagger-ingly support some idea of giving things which cannot be demanded and avoiding things which cannot be punished? Our only claim is to be a wall across Christendom against the Jew pedlars and pawnbrokers, against the Goldsteins and the—"

The Duke of Aylesbury swung round with his hands in his pockets.

"Oh, I say," he said, "you've been readin' Lloyd George. Nobody but dirty Radicals can say a word against Goldstein."

"I certainly cannot permit," said the elder Duke, rising rather shakily, "the respected name of Lord Goldstein—"

He intended to be impressive, but there was something in the Fren-chman's eye that is not so easily impressed; there shone there that steel which is the mind of France.

"Gentlemen," he said, "I think I have all the details now. You have ruled England for four hundred years. By your own account you have not made the countryside endurable to men. By your own ac-count you have helped the victory of vulgarity and smoke. And by your own account you are hand and glove with those very money-grubbers and adventurers whom gentlemen have no other business but to keep at bay. I do not know what your people will do; but my people would kill you.''

Some seconds afterwards he had left the Duke's house, and some hours afterwards the Duke's estate.

The Roots of the World

Once upon a time a little boy lived in a garden in which he was permitted to pick the flowers but forbidden to pull them up by the roots. There was, however, one particular plant, insignificant, somewhat thorny, with a small, star-like flower, which he very much wanted to pull up by the roots. His tutors and guardians, who lived in the house with him, were worthy, formal people, and they gave him reasons why he should not pull it up. They were silly reasons as a rule. But none of the reasons against doing the thing was quite so silly as the little boy's reason for wanting to do it; for his reason was that Truth demanded that he should pull the thing up by the roots to see how it was growing. Still it was a sleepy, thoughtless kind of house, and nobody gave him the real answer to his argument, which was that it would kill the plant, and that there is no more Truth about a dead plant than about a live one. So one dark night, when clouds sealed the moon like a secret too good or too bad to be told, the little boy came down the old creaking stairs of his farmhouse and crept into the garden in his nightgown. He told himself repeatedly that there was no more reason against his pulling this plant off the garden than against his knocking off a thistle-top idly in a lane. Yet the darkness which he had chosen contradicted him, and also his own throbbing pulse, for he told himself continually that next morning he might be crucified as the blasphemer who had torn up the sacred tree.

Perhaps he might have been so crucified if he had so torn it up. I cannot say. But he did not tear it up; and it was not for want of trying. For when he laid hold of the little plant in the garden he tugged and tugged, and found the thing held as if clamped to the earth with iron. And when he strained himself a third time there came a frightful noise behind him, and either nerves or (which he would have denied) conscience made him leap back and stagger and stare around. The house he lived in was a mere bulk of blackness against a sky almost as black. Yet after staring long he saw that the very outline had grown unfamiliar, for the great chimney of the kitchen had fallen crooked and calamitous. Desperately he gave another pull at the plant, and heard far off the roof of the stables fall in and the horses shriek and plunge. Then he ran into the house and rolled himself in the bedclothes. Next morning found the kitchen ruined, the day's food destroyed, two horses dead, and three broken loose and lost. But the boy still kept a furious curiosity, and a little while after, when a fog from the sea had hidden house and garden, he dragged again at the roots of the indestructable plant. He hung on to it like a boy on the rope of a tug of war, but it did not give. Only through the grey sea-fog came choking and panic-stricken cries; they cried that the King's castle had fallen, that the towers guarding the coast were gone; that half the great sea-city had split away and slid into the sea. Then the boy was frightened for a little while, and said no more about the plant, but when he had come to a strong and careless manhood. and the destruction in the district had been repaired, he said openly before the people, "Let us have done with the riddle of this irrational weed. In the name of Truth let us drag it up." And he gathered a great company of strong men, like an army to meet invaders, and they all laid hold of the little plant and they tugged night and day. And the Great Wall fell down in China for forty miles. And the Pyramids were split up into jagged stones. And the Eiffel Tower in Paris went over like a ninepin, killing half the Parisians; and the Statue of Liberty in New York harbour fell forward suddenly and smashed the American fleet; and St. Paul's Cathedral killed all the journalists in Fleet Street, and Japan had a record series of earthquakes and then sank into the sea. Some have declared that these last two incidents were not calamities properly so called; but into that I will not enter. The point was that when they had tugged for about twenty-four hours the strong men of that country had pulled down about half of the civilized world, but had not pulled up the plant. I will not weary the reader with the full facts of this realistic story, with how they used first elephants and then steam-engines to tear up the flower, and how the only result was that the flower stuck fast, but that the moon began to be agitated and even the sun was a bit dicky. At last the human race interfered, as it always does at last, by means of a revolution. But long before that the boy, or man, who is the hero of this tale, had thrown up the business, merely saying to his pastors and masters, "You gave me a number of elaborate and idle reasons why I should not pull up this shrub. Why did you not give me the two good reasons; first, that I can't; second, that I should damage everything else if I ever tried it on?"

Chivalry Begins At Home

Mr. William Hicks of West Kensington rose from breakfast, giving the morning paper a flourish as if it were a flag. A new light was in his eyes; he had been fired by the the appeal of Mr. Mitchell-Hedges and his demand for a return of the old English spirit of adventure, as shown by explorers and pioneers. A moment's reflection showed him that adventure was difficult for a clerk with a small salary; for it seemed to cost a good deal to "fit out" an expedition. Adventure, which would seem to be the cheapest thing, is really the most expensive. And then a second and more reasonable reflection occurred to him. The essential of the explorer's appeal was to energy and courage, to seeking peril and experience, not latitude and longitude. After all, an adventurous life can be lived anywhere, so long as there is danger and an honourable cause.

His next-door neighbour, who had furnished his house on the hire system, had indeed paid the whole of the highly profiteering price in instalments, save for a few shillings, and had then lost everything, both the money and the furniture, and been practically ruined. The neighbour was ready enough to say it was a swindle, as it was. None the less was he somewhat surprised at the appearance of Mr. Hicks climbing by moonlight over the garden wall, with a mask, a pistol, a jemmy and a rope-ladder and a proposal to recover the furniture from the neighbouring warehouse by burglary. Mr. Hicks was surprised by the sudden cooling of the spirit of adventure in the victim of oppression; for, as he pointed out, the cause was more just than that against any savage tribe and the peril defied far greater than that of lions.

Mr. Hicks was arrested by the police when halfway down a rope with the third bedroom chair in his teeth. Seldom, he admitted, had he felt so much the thrill of adventure. He received a short sentence as a first offender; a defect that he at once set about to correct. Proceeding to the mansion of a usurer, he fought with three footmen and a butler on the way to deliver his denunciation and was eventually arrested again for demanding money with threats. But he was so stubborn and pertinacious in his course that it seemed more safe and scientific to convict him of being feeble-minded. Finding himself shut up in an asylum with several people as sane as himself, he raised a mutiny, put all the doctors into strait waistcoats and fled to London. He resolved to attack head-quarters, and by climbing on the roof of Downing Street and coming down the chimney, he presented himself before a Cabinet Minister, a pleasant, rather humorous-looking man, smoking a pipe after dinner. Indeed his reception was so disarmingly genial that he found himself speaking warmly in his own defence: "What does it mean?" he demanded. "You all praise courage and adventure; all your novels are full of it; all your newspapers urge us to it, saying the pioneers are the only patriots. Why do you praise all these adventurers in distant lands?"

"Precisely," said the politician with a smile. "In distant lands. Don't you think you've answered your own question, Mr. Hicks? Or must you be let in to a little more of the secret? My dear sir, adventure is a great thing, a glorious thing; and why? Because it kills off adventurous people. Empire-Building at the ends of the earth is splendid, and why? Because it keeps all adventurers out of the country — just like undesirable aliens. Patriots — yes, indeed; have you never understood the pathos of those lovely lines: 'True patriots they, for be it understood they left their country for their country's good.' "

The statesman's smile was rather subtle: and Mr. Hicks left the house thoughtfully, not by the chimney but the door.

The Sword Of Wood

Down in the little village of Grayling-Abbot, in Somerset, men did not know that the world we live in had begun. They did not know that all we have come to call 'modern' had silently entered England, and changed the air of it. Well, they did not know it very clearly even in London: though one or two shrewd men like my Lord Clarendon, and perhaps Prince Rupert, with his chemicals and his sad eyes, may have had a glimmer of it.

On the contrary, by the theory of the thing, the old world had returned. Christmas could be kept again; the terrible army was disbanded; the swarthy young man with the sour, humorous face, who had been cheered from Dover to Whitehall, brought back in him the blood of kings. Every one was saying (especially in Grayling-Abbot) that now it would be Merry England again. But the swarthy young man knew better. The Merry Monarch knew he was not meant to make Merry England. If he treated his own life as a comedy, it was for a philosophical reason; because comedy is the only poetry of compromise. And he was a compromise; and he knew it. Therefore he turned, like Prince Rupert, to the chemicals; and played with the little toys that were to become the terrible engines of modern science. So he might have played with tiger-cubs, so long as they were as small as his spaniels.

But down in Grayling-Abbot it was much easier to believe that old England had been restored, because it had never, in any serious sense, been disturbed. The fierce religious quarrels of the seventeenth century had only stirred that rustic neighbourhood to occasional panics of witch-burning. And these, though much rarer in the medieval society, were not inconsistent with it. The squire, Sir Guy Griffin, was famous as a fighter quite in the medieval style. Though he had commanded a troop under Newcastle in the Civil Wars with conspicuous success, the local legend of his bodily prowess eclipsed any national chronicle of his military capacity. Through two or three counties round Grayling-Abbot, his reputation for swordsmanship had quite eclipsed his reputation for generalship. So, in the Middle Ages, it happened that Coeur-de-Lion's hand could keep his head: it happened that Bruce's hand could keep his head. And in both cases the head has suffered unfairly from the glorification of the hand.

The same almost unbroken medieval tradition even clung round the young schoolmaster, Dennis Tryon, who was just locking up his little school for the last time; having been transferred to a private post at Sir Guy's own house, to teach Sir Guy's six hulking sons, who had learned their father's skill with the sword, and hitherto declined to learn anything else. In numberless and nameless ways, Tryon expressed the old traditions. He was not a Puritan, yet he wore black clothes because he might have been a priest. Though he had learned to fence and dance at College, like Milton, he was plainly dressed and weaponless; because the vague legend remained that a student was a sort of clerk, and a clerk was a sort of clergyman. He wore his brown hair long, like a Cavalier. But as it was his own hair, it was long and straight: while the Cavaliers were already beginning to wear other people's hair, which was long and curly. In that strict brown frame, his face had the boyish, frank, rather round appearance that may be seen in old miniatures of Falkland or the Duke of Monmouth. His favourite authors were George Herbert and Sir Thomas Browne; and he was very young.

He was addressing a last word to a last pupil, who happened to be lingering outside the school — a minute boy of seven, playing with one of those wooden swords, made of two lengths of lath nailed across each other, which boys have played with in all centuries.

"Jeremy Bunt," said Tyron, with a rather melancholy playfulness, "your sword is, as it seems to me, much an improvement on most we have lately looked on. I observe its end is something blunt; doubtless for that gallant reason that led Orlando to blunt his sword when fighting the lady, whose name, in the ingenious romance, escapes me. Let it suffice you, little one. It will kill the Giants, like Master Jack's sword of sharpness, at least as well as the swords of a standing army ever will. If you be minded to save the Lady Angelica from the ogre, it will turn the dragon to stone as quick as any sword of steel would do. And, oh, Jeremy, if the fable be false, the moral is not false. If a little boy be good and brave, he should be great, and he may be. If he be bad and base, he should be beaten with a staff " — here Tryon tapped him very softly on the shoulders with a long black walking-cane that was commonly his only ferule — "but in either way, to my thinking, your sword is as good as any other. Only, dear Jeremy" — and he bent over the child swiftly, with a sudden tenderness — " always remember your kind of sword is stronger if one holds it by the wrong end."

He reversed the little sword in the child's hand, making it a wooden cross, and then went striding up the road like the wind, leaving the staring boy behind.

When he became conscious that human feet were following him, he knew they could not possibly be the feet of the boy. He looked round; and Jeremy was still hovering in the distance; but the rush of feet came from a far different cause.

A young lady was hurrying by close under the high hedge that was nearly as old as the Plantagenets. Her costume was like his own, in the sense that it had the quietude of the Puritan with the cut of the Cavalier. Her dress was as dark as Barebones could have asked; but the ringlets under her hood were yellow and curly, for the same reason that his own hair was brown and straight: because they were her own. Nothing else was notable about her, except that she was pretty and seemed rather in a hurry; and that her delicate profile was pointed resolutely up the road. The face was a little pale.

Tryon turned again to look back on his tracks; and this time saw another figure more formidable than Jeremy with the wooden sword.

A tall, swaggering figure, almost black against the sunlight, was coming down the road with a rapidity that almost amounted to a run. He had a wide hat with feathers, and long, luxuriant hair, in the latest London manner; but it was not any such feathers or flourishes that arrested Tryon's attention. He had seen old Sir Guy Griffin, who still wore his wild, white hair half-way down his back, to show (very unnecessarily) that he was not a Puritan. He had seen Sir Guy stick in his hat the most startling cock's feathers, but that was because he had no other feathers. But Tryon knew at a glance that Sir Guy would never have come forward in such extraordinary attitudes. The tall, fantastic man actually drew his sword as he rushed forward; and offered it like a lance to be splintered as from the end of a long tilting-yard. Such frolics may have happened a hundred times round the 'Cock' of Buckingham and Dorset. But it was an action utterly unknown to the gentry round Grayling-Abbot, when they settled affairs of honour.

While he was still looking up the road at the advancing figure, he found himself breathlessly addressed by the escaping girl.

"You must not fight him," she said, "he has beaten everybody. He has beaten even Sir Guy, and all his sons." She cast her eyes about him and cried out in horror: "And where is your sword?"

"With my spurs, mistress," replied the schoolmaster, in the best style of Ariosto. "I have to win them both."

She looked at him rather wildly and said: "But he has never been beaten in swordsmanship."

Tryon, with a smile, made a salute with his black walking-stick. "A man with no sword," he said, "can never be beaten in swordsmanship."

The girl stood for one moment staring at him as if, even in that scene of scurry and chase, time were suspended for a flash. Then she seemed to leap again like a hunted thing and plunged on: and it was only some hundred yards higher up the road that she again halted, hesitated, and looked back. In much the same manner Master Jeremy Bunt, who had not the faintest intention of deserting the delightful school in which he was no longer required to do any work, actually ran forward. Perhaps their curiosity ought to be excused. For they were certainly looking at the most astounding duel the world had ever seen. It was the duel of the naked sword and the walking-stick: probably the only merely defensive battle ever fought on this earth.

The day was full of sun and wind, the two chief ingredients of a glorious day; but till that moment even Mr. Tryon, though of a pastoral and poetical turn, had not noticed anything specially splendid in the sky or landscape. Now the beauty of this world came upon him with the violence of a supernatural vision; for he was very certain it was a vision that he soon must lose. He was a good fencer with the foil in the Collegiate manner. But it was not to be expected that any human being could emerge victorious from a prolonged fight in which he had no means of retaliation; and especially as his opponent, whether from drink or devilry, was clearly fighting to the death. Tryon could not be certain that the wild creature even knew that his sword only struck against wood.

Dennis Tryon took in every glory of the good English land, and the

still more glorious English climate, with the corner of his eye; he took
it in with that same swift, indirect and casual, yet absolutely substantial
way in which Nature is noticed in the old English poets that he loved.
For the great poets of England, from Chaucer to Dryden, had a trick
that has since been lost, the trick of implying the nature of a scene
without apparently even attempting to describe it. Thus, any one
reading the line "Pack, clouds, away," knows at once it is the kind
of clouds called *cumuli*, and could not possibly be meant for level or
streaky clouds. Or any one reading Milton's line about the princess's
turret 'bosomed high in tufted trees' knows it means partly leafless
trees, as in early spring or autumn, when the edge of the forest shows
soft against the sky, like a brush or broom, sweeping heaven. With
the same sort of subconscious solidity, Tryon realized the rounded
and half-rosy morning clouds that curled or huddled in the blue above
the downs; and the mute mercy of the forests, that faded from grey
to purple before they mixed with heaven. Death, in a hat with black
plumes, was shooting a thousand shining arrows at him every instant;
and he had never loved the world so much before.

For indeed that one streak of white steel came at him like a shower of
shining arrows. He had to make a new parry for every new lunge; and,
with each, perversely remembered some episode of College fencing.
When the bright point of death missed his heart and slid past his
elbow, he saw suddenly a meadow beside the Thames. When he seemed blinded, by the very light on that lightning blade, leaping at his eyes
but passing over his shoulder, he saw the old lawn at Merton as if
its grass had sprung out of the road around him. But he began more
and more to realize something else. He realized that if he had held
a real sword, he could have killed his enemy six times over with the
riposte. When the heart-thrust was turned, he could have put his sword
like a carving-knife into a pudding — if it had been a sword. When
the parry protected his eyes, nothing else could have protected his
opponent, except the unpenetrating quality of a walking-stick. His
brain was of the very clear kind that can play two games of chess at
once. While still whirling his black walking-stick in a complicated
but impromptu clockwork of fence, he saw quite clearly a logical alter-
native. Either the man thought he was fighting someone with a sword:
in which case he was a very bad fencer. Or else he knew he was fighting

someone with a stick, in which case he was a very bad man: or (as
the more timid modern phrase goes) a very bad sportsman.

He acted suddenly in a way adapted to either case. He introduced
into his swordplay a stroke of single-stick, also learned at College,
jerking his stick up so as to strike and jar the man's elbow; and then,
before the arm could recover its nerve, smote the sword clean out
of the hand. A look at the man's black, bewildered expression was
enough. Tryon was now quite certain the man's advantage had only
been in his sword. He was also quite certain the man knew it. With
all the rush of his released romanticism, which roared like the wind,
and rolled like the clouds, and blazed like the sun which he had
thought to see no more, he sprang forward and pinned the man by
the throat, with a shout of laughter. Then he said, with more restrained
humour, what he had said to the little boy up the road.

"If he be bad and base," said Tryon, "he should be beaten with
a staff." And whirling the walking-stick round his head, he laid three
thundering and echoing thwacks across the shoulders of his disarm-
ed enemy, and walked off up the road again like the wind.

He did not notice further what his murderous enemy might attempt,
but he was honestly puzzled about the conduct of the crowd. For,
by this time, there was a very considerable crowd. The sword-bearing
Jeremy was quite prominent in the throng behind him; the lady with
the golden curls and the sensitive profile was herself pausing a
moment on the outskirts of the throng in front.

As he started up the road again, the mob set up a roar, redoubled
and quadrupled, and several gentlemen present whirled their plum-
ed hats and shouted observations he could not hear. What was even
more extraordinary, a great part of the crowd (including the young
lady, who vanished early) appeared to be disappearing up the road,
as if bringing news of some great victory like Agincourt.

By the time he came from Grayling-Abbot to Grayling-le-Griffin,
the next village, there were ten heads at every cottage window; and
girls threw flowers, that missed him and fell on the road. By the time
he came to the outskirts of the Park, with the stone griffins, there
were triumphal arches.

"It seems that I was not a little hasty with Master Bunt," said Tryon
to himself, with a puzzled smile. "It is plain I have fallen into the

Kingdom of Queen Mab. It is I, and not Master Jeremy, who have, in some sense, saved Angelica from the dragon. I was rather more embarrassed in the matter of arms, and she rather less embarrassed in the matter of attire, and there, truly, the difference seems to end. But the strangest thing of all is that, whatever I have done, I have done it with a sword of wood, like little Jeremy's.''

In his academic reflections, he lifted his long black stick to look at it; and, as he did so, the cry of many crowds broke about him like a cannonade. For he had come to the very doors of Griffin Grange, to which he had been summoned on his much milder tutorial errand. And the great Sir Guy himself came out at the entrance. He might even have justified his mythic name, allowing for certain alterations of accident. For a griffin was supposed to be a mixture of the lion and the eagle; and certainly Sir Guy's mane might have been a lion's, but that it was largely white; and his nose might have been an eagle's, but that it was partly red.

His face had at first a dangerous and even dissipated look, and Tryon had one momentary doubt about the reason of his defeat. But when he looked again at Sir Guy's erect figure and animated eye; when he rather timidly accepted his decisive handshake and received congratulations in his clear and comfortable voice, the doubt vanished. And the young schoolmaster felt even more bewildered in receiving the equally adoring, though rather more gaping, congratulations of the six strenuous sons. At the first glance, Tryon felt something like despair about their Greek and Latin. But he also felt an increasing conviction that any of them could have knocked him anywhere with a cudgel. His own triumph began to seem as fantastic and incredible as his triumphal arches.

"Assuredly it is a strange matter," he said to himself in his simplicity. "I was a tolerable good fencer at Merton, but not excellent. Not so good as Wilton or Smith or old King of Christ Church. It is not to be believed that men like these could not beat him with their great swords, when I could beat him with a stick. This is some jest of the great gentry, as in the ingenious tale of Master Cervantes."

He therefore received the uproarious plaudits of old Griffin and his sons with some reserve; but, after a little time, it was hard for one so simple not to perceive their simplicity. They really did regard him, as little Jeremy would have regarded him, as a fairy-tale hero who had freed their valley from an ogre. The people at the windows had not been conspirators. The triumphal arches had not been practical jokes. He was really the god of the countryside and he had not a notion why.

Three things convinced him finally of the reality of his reputation. One was the mysterious fact that the young Griffins (that brood of mythic monsters) really made some attempt to learn. Humphrey, the eldest and biggest, got the genitive of *quis* right the third time, though wrong again the fourth, fifth, and sixth. The attempts of Geoffrey to distinguish between *fingo* and *figo* would have moved a heart of stone; and Miles, the youngest, was really interested in the verb *ferre*, though (being a waterside character) he had some tendency to end it with a 'y'. Underneath all this exceptional mental ambition, Tryon could see the huge, silent respect which savages and schoolboys feel everywhere for one who has 'done' something in the bodily way. The old rural and real aristocracy of England had not that rather cold and clumsy class-consciousness we now call the public-school spirit; and they enjoyed sports instead of worshipping them. But boys are the same in all ages, and one of their sports is hero-worship.

The next and yet more fascinating fact was Sir Guy. He was not, it was clear, in the common sense an amiable man. Just as the slash he had at the battle of Newbury made his eagle face almost as ugly as it was handsome, so the neglects and disappointments of his once promising military career had made his tongue and temper as bitter as they were sincere. Yet Tryon felt he owed the very knowledge of such an attitude to a confidence the old man would not have reposed in other people.

"The King hath his own again," old Griffin would say gloomily. "But I think it is too late. Indeed it might nigh as well be the King of France come to rule us as the King of England. He hath brought back with him French women that act in stage plays as if they were boys; and tricks fit for pothecaries or conjurers at a fair, and tricks like this fellow's that twitched away my sword, and every one else's — till he met his master, thank God." And he smiled at Tryon, sourly, but with respect.

"Is the gentleman I met," asked Tryon, rather timidly, "one from the Court?"

"Yes," answered the old man. "Did you look at his face?"

"Only his eyes," said the fencer, smiling; "they are black."

"His face is painted," said Griffin. "That is the sort of thing they do in London. And he wears a pile of false hair out of a barber's; and walks about in it, like the house of a Jack-in-the-Green. But his was the best sword, as old Noll's was the best army. And what could we do?"

The third fact, which affected Dennis Tryon most deeply of all, was a glimpse or two of the girl he had saved from the obstreperous courtier. It appeared she was the parson's daughter, one Dorothy Hood, who was often in and out of the Grange, but always avoided him. He had every sort of delicacy himself; and a comprehension of her attitude made him finally certain of his own inexplicable importance. If this had been, as he first thought, a trick played on him in the style of the Duke and the Tinker, so charming a girl (and he thought her more charming every time she flashed down a corridor or disappeared through a door) would certainly have been set to draw him on. If there was a conspiracy, she must be in it; and her part in it would be plain. But she was not playing the part. He caught himself rather wishing she were.

The last stroke came when he heard her saying to Sir Guy, by the accident of two open doors: "All say, 'twas witchcraft; and that God helped the young gentleman only because he was good, and — "

He walked wildly away. He was the kind of academic cavalier, who had learnt all worldly manners in an unworldly cloister. To him, therefore, eavesdropping was in all cases, horrible; in her case, damnable.

On one occasion he plucked up his courage to stop and thank her for having warned him of the danger of the duel.

Her delicate, pale face, always tremulous, became positively troubled. "But then I did not know" she said. "I knew you were not afraid. But I did not know then you were fighting the devils."

"Truly, and I do not know it now," he answered. "By my thinking, I was fighting one man, and no such great fighting at that."

"Everybody says it was the devils," she said with a beautiful simplicity. "My father says so."

When she had slipped away, Dennis was left meditating: and a new and rather grim impression grew stronger and stronger upon him. The more he heard from servants or strangers, the clearer it was that the local legend was hardening into a tale of himself as exorcist breaking the spell of a warlock.

The youngest boy, Miles, who had been (as usual) down by the river, said the villagers were walking along the bank, looking for the old pool where witches were drowned. Humphrey said it would be no good if they found it, for the tall man with the painted face had gone back to London. But an hour later, Geoffrey came in with other news: the wicked wizard had gone out of Grayling, but the mob had stopped him on the road to Salisbury.

When Tryon bestirred himself with curiosity and alarm and looked out of the Grange gates he found fearful confirmation, almost in the image of a place of pestilence or a city of the dead. The whole population of the two villages of Grayling (save for such non-combatants as the wooden-sworded Bunt) had vanished from their streets and houses. They returned in the dark hour before dawn; and they brought with them the man with the magic sword.

Men in modern England, who have never seen a revolution, who have never seen even a real mob, cannot imagine what the capture of a witch was like. It was for all the populace of that valley a vast rising against an emperor and oppressor, a being taller, more terrible, more universal, than any one would have called either Charles I or Cromwell, even in jest. It was not, as the modern people say, the worrying of some silly old woman. It was for them a revolt against Kehama, the Almighty Man. It was for them a rebellion of the good angels after the victory of Satan. Dorothy Hood was sufficiently frightened of the mob to take Tryon's hand in the crowd, and hold it in a way that made them understand each other with an intimate tenderness never afterwards dissolved. But it never occurred to her to be sorry for the warlock.

He was standing on the river bank, with his hands tied behind him, but the sword still at his side; no one feeling disposed to meddle with it. His peruke had been torn off; and his cropped head seemed to make more glaring and horrible the unnatural colours of his face. It was like some painted demon mask. But he was quite composed, and even contemptuous. Every now and then people threw things at him, as

at one in the pillory; even little Jeremy Bunt flinging his wooden
sword, with all the enthusiasm of the Children's Crusade. But most
things missed him and fell into the flowing river behind, into which
(there could be little doubt) he himself was to be flung at last.

Then stood up for an instant in the stormy light, that rare but real
spirit, for whose sake alone men have endured aristocracy, or the divi-
sion of man from man. Sir Guy's scarred face looked rather unusually
sulky, or even spiteful; but he turned to his bodyguard of sons. "We
must get him back safe to the Grange," he said sourly; "you boys
have all your swords, I think. You had best draw them."

"Why?" asked the staring Humphrey.

"Why," answered his father, "because they are conquered swords,
like my own." And he drew his long blade, that took the white light
of the morning.

"Boys," he said, "it is in the hand of God if he be warlock or no.
But is it to be said of our blood that we brought crowds and clubs
to kill a man who had whipped each one of us fairly with the sword?
Shall men say that when Griffins met their match they whined about
magic? Make a ring round him, and we will bring him alive through
a thousand witch-smellers."

Already a half-ring of naked swords had swung round the victim
like a spiked necklace. In those days mobs were much bolder against
their masters than they are to-day. But even that mob gave to the
Griffins a military reputation beyond their mere territorial rank; and
the parties were thus the more equal. There was no sword in that
crowd better than a Griffin sword; except the sword that hung useless
at the hip of a pinioned man.

Before the next moment, which must have been blood and destruction, the man with the useless sword spoke. "If some gentleman,"
he said with marmoreal calm, "will but put a hand in the pocket of
my doublet, I think bloodshed will be spared."

There was a long silence; and every one looked at Dennis Tryon:
the man who had not feared the wizard. Every one included Dorothy;
and Dennis stepped forward. He found a folded piece of paper in the
doublet, opened it and read it with more and more wonder on his
round young face. At the third sentence he took his hat off. At this
the crowd stared more and more: it had fallen suddenly silent and

all were conscious of a change and a cooling in that intense air.

"It would appear," he said at last, "that this is a privy letter from His Majesty, which I will not read in entirety. But it advises and permits Sir Godfrey Skene to practise with the new Magnetic Sword which the Royal Society has for some little time attempted to manufacture in pursuance of a suggestion of Lord Verulam, the founder of our Natural Philosophy. The whole blade is magnetized; and it is thought it may even pull any other iron weapon out of the hand."

He paused a moment, in some embarrassment, and then said: "It is added that only a weapon of wood or such other material could be used against it."

Sir Guy turned to him suddenly and said: "Is that what you call Natural Philosophy?"

"Yes," replied Tryon.

"I thank you," said Griffin. "You need not teach it to my sons."

Then he strode towards the prisoner, and rent the sword away, bursting the belt that held it.

"If it were not His Majesty's own hand," he said, "I would throw you with it after all."

The next instant the Magnetic Sword of the Royal Society vanished from men's view for ever; and Tryon could see nothing but Jeremy's little cross of wood heaving with the heaving stream.

PART THREE
Utopias Unlimited

The Dragon at Hide-and-Seek

Once upon a time there was a knight who was an outlaw, that is a man hiding from the king and everybody else; and one who lived so wild and lawless a life, in being hunted from one hiding-place to another, that he had great difficulty in going to church every Sunday. Although his ordinary way of life was full of fighting, and burning, and breaking down doors, and therefore looked a little careless, he had been very carefully brought up, and it was obviously a very serious thing that he should be late for church. But he was so clever and daring in his way of getting from one place to another without being caught, that he generally managed it somehow. And it was often a considerable disturbance to the congregation when he came with a great crash flying in through the big stained-glass window and smashing it to atoms, having been patiently hanging on a gargoyle outside for half an hour; or, when he dropped suddenly out of the belfry, where he had been hiding in one of the big bells, and alighted almost on the heads of the worshippers. Nor were they better pleased when he preferred to dig a hole in the churchyard and crawl under the church-wall, coming up suddenly under a lifted paving-stone in the middle of the nave or the chancel. They were too well-behaved, of course, to notice the incident during the service; and the more just among them admitted that even outlaws must get to church somehow; but it caused a certain amount of talk in the town, and the history of the knight and his wonderful way of hiding everywhere and anywhere was by this time familiar to the whole country-side. At last this knight, who was called Sir Laverok, began to feel so sure of his power of escaping and hiding, whenever he wanted to, that he would come into the market-place in the most inpudent manner when any great business was being transacted, such as the elections of the guilds, or even to the coronation of the King, to whom he addressed some well-chosen words of advice about his public duties, in a loud voice from the chimney-pot of an adjoining house. Often, when the King and his lords were out hunting, or even when they were in camp during a great war, they would look up and see Sir Laverok perched like a bird on a tree above their heads, and ever ready with friendly counsels and almost fatherly good wishes. But though they pursued him with emotions of uninterrupted rage, lasting over several months, they were never able to discover what were the holes and corners in which he hid himself. They were forced to admit that his talent for disappearing into undiscovered places was of the highest order, and that in a children's game of Hide-and-Seek he would have covered himself with everlasting glory; but they all felt that a fugitive from justice should be strictly forbidden to cultivate genius of this kind.

Now it was just about this time that there fell upon the whole of that country an enormous calamity far worse than any war or pestilence. It was a kind which we have very few chances of experiencing nowadays; though in the other matter of wars and diseases our opportunities are still wide and varied. There had appeared in the wilderness to the north of that country, a monster of huge size and horrible habits and disposition; a monster who might have been called, for the sake of simplicity, a dragon, only he had feet like an elephant, but a hundred times bigger, with which he used to stamp and crush everything to a flat and fine paste before he licked it up with a tongue as long and large as the Great Sea Serpent; and his great jaws opened wide like a whale's, only that they could have swallowed a shoal of whales as if they were whitebait. No weapons or missiles seemed to be of any avail against him; for his skin was plated with iron of incredible thickness. Indeed, some declared that he was entirely composed of iron, and that he had been made out of that material by a magician who lived beyond the wilderness, where such crafts and spells were more seriously studied. Indeed, it was hinted by some that the land of the magicians was in every way in advance of their own, and well worthy of emulation; and that if anyone objected that this marvellous machinery had no apparent effect except in killing people and destroying beautiful things, he should be rebuked as one lacking in enterprise and a larger outlook upon the future. But those who said this, commonly said it before they had actually met the new animal, and it was noticed that after meeting him they seldom uttered these thoughts, or, indeed, any other.

The monster may have been made of iron, and his nerves and muscles may have been, as some said, made like an arrangement of wheels and wires, but he was most unmistakably alive; and proved it by having a hearty appetite and an evident enjoyment of life. He trampled and devoured first, all the fortifications of the frontier, and then the castles and the larger towns of the interior; and by the time that he was marching towards the capital, the King and his courtiers were all climbing to the tops of towers, and everybody else to the tops of trees. These precautions proved inadequate in practical experience; in very practical experience. So long as the monster could be seen twenty miles away like a marching mountain, already fantastic in outline, but still blue or purple with distance, and there was no other sign of him except a slight shaking of the houses as in a mild earthquake, these conjectures and expedients could be debated copiously, if not always calmly. But when the creature came near enough for his habits to be closely studied, it was clear that he could tread down trees like grass, and flatten out castles like houses of cards. It became more and more the fashion to seek out less showy and more secluded country resorts; the whole population, led by magistrates, merchants, and all its natural leaders, fleeing with startling rapidity to the mountains and concealing themselves in holes and caverns, which they blocked behind them with big rocks. Even this was not very successful; the monster proceeded to scale the mountains with the gaiety of a goat, to kick the rocky barricades to pieces, letting in daylight on the cowering company within; and many of them were able to recognize the familiar shape of the long and curling tongue of the intelligent creature, exploring their retreat and coiling and twisting and darting about in a very playful and sportive manner. Those who had not found any hole to crawl into, and who were clinging in crowds to the crags higher up the hill, were at this moment, however, surprised with a sight that almost took their thoughts for an instant off the universal peril. On the highest crag of all, above their heads, had appeared suddenly the figure of Sir Laverok with his old spear in his hand, with his sword girt around his ragged armour, and the wind waving about his wild hair that was the colour of flame. In all that huddling crowd it was only the man in hiding who stood out conspicuous; and only the man fleeing from justice who did not flee.

"I am not afraid," he said in answer to their wild cries. "You know I have a trick of finding my way to places of safety. And as it happens, I know a castle to which I shall retreat, and to which the dragon can never come."

"But, my good Sir," said the Chancellor, pausing in the act of trying to creep into a rabbit-burrow, "the dragon can grind castles to powder with his heel. I regret to say that he showed not the least embarrassment even in approaching the Law Courts."

"I know of a castle which he cannot reach," said Sir Laverok.

"The offensive animal," said the Lord Chamberlain, poking his head for a moment out of a hole in the ground, "actually entered the King's private chamber without knocking."

"I know of a private chamber that he cannot enter," replied the outlaw knight.

"It is very doubtful," came the muffled voice of the Lord High Admiral from somewhere underground, "whether we shall even be safe in any of the caverns."

"I know a cavern where I shall be safe," said Sir Laverok.

At the foot of the steep slope to which they clung spread a large plateau like a plain; and over this bare tableland, at the moment, the monster was prowling up and down like a polar bear, considering what he would destroy next. Every time he turned his head towards them, the crowds clambered a little higher up the hill; but they soon saw, to their astonishment, that Sir Laverok was not climbing up, but climbing down. He dropped from the last overhanging rock, and rushed out upon the plain against the monster; when he came within a short distance, the knight gave one wild leap and threw his spear like a thunderbolt.

What happened in the flash of that thunderbolt nobody in the crowd seemed to know. Those who knew them best were of the opinion that they all shut their eyes tight, and most probably fell flat on their faces. Others say that the monster stamped his foot upon his enemy with so stunning a shock that a cloud of dust rolled up to the clouds of heaven, and for a moment hid the whole scene. Others, again, explained that the vast immeasurable bulk of the monster had come between them and the victim. Anyhow, it is certain that when that vast bulk turned once more and began swaying and lurching backwards and forwards on its lonely prowl, no sign of the victim could be seen. Probably he had been stamped to mire as everything else had been.

But if it were conceivable that he had indeed escaped, as he had boasted, it was hard to say where; as there did not seem to be anywhere for him to escape to. And the authorities in the holes and caves could not but regret that they had not condemned him to be burned as a wizard instead of hanged as a rebel, whenever they should have put the final touch to the sentence by carrying it into effect. They comforted themselves in the cave by the reflection that at least no hasty capture or premature execution had yet put it out of their power to rectify the mistake; but for the moment it seemed clear that their chances either of hanging or burning the gentleman were further off than ever.

Just at that moment, however, there was a new interruption. It so happened that the King's third daughter was standing in the crowd on the slope; for all the elder members of the royal family were enjoying a temporary and semi-official retirement from the cares of state at the bottom of a dry well on the other side of the mountain range. But she had been unable or unwilling to travel with the extreme rapidity which they had had the presence of mind to exhibit; for she was rather an absent-minded person, wholly without aptitude for practical politics. She was called the Princess Philomel, and was a dreamy sort of person, with long hair and blue eyes that were like the blue of distant horizons, and she was commonly very silent; but she had watched the adventure of the vanishing outlaw with more interest than she commonly showed in anything; and she startled everybody at this stage by breaking her silence and calling out in a clear voice:

"Yes; he has found his fairy castle where no dragon can come."

The more dignified Councillors of State were just venturing to put their noses above ground in order to remonstrate respectfully against the breach of etiquette, when everybody's attention was again distracted to the monster, who was behaving in an even more extraordinary way than usual. Instead of pacing backwards and forwards with a certain pomposity as he had done before, he was bounding to and fro, taking totally unnecessary leaps into the air and clawing in a most uncomfortable and inconsequent fashion.

"What is the matter with him now?" enquired the Master of the Buckhounds, who was something of a student of animal life, and would, under other circumstances, have been much interested in the phenomenon.

"The monster is angry," replied the Princess Philomel in the same absolute if abstracted fashion. "He is angry because the knight has reached the magic chamber and cannot be found."

If the monster was indeed exhibiting anger, it would seem that his anger had an element of self-reproach. For he was evidently clawing and scratching at himself rather in the manner of a dog hunting a flea, but much more savagely.

"Can he be killing himself?" asked the Lord Chancellor hopefully. "I am the keeper of the King's conscience, and not, of course, the keeper of the dragon's. But it seems possible that his conscience, if once aroused, would find in retrospect some legitimate ground for remorse."

"Nonsense," said the Chamberlain, "why should he kill himself?"

"If it comes to that," answered the other, "why should he fight himself, as he seems to be doing?"

"Because," answered the Princess, "Sir Laverok has at last reached the cavern where he is safe."

But even as she spoke, a further and final change seemed to pass over the monster. For a moment it looked as if he had turned into two or three different monsters, for the different parts of him were behaving in different ways. One hind leg rested as calmly on the earth as the column of a temple, while the other was kicking wildly up behind and thrashing the air like the sail of a windmill. One eye was standing out of the head in hideous prominence, and rolling round and round like a catherine-wheel of fury, while the other was already closed with the placid expression of a cow who had gone to sleep. Then the next moment both eyes were closed, and both feet stationary, and the whole monster, with a deprecating expression, turned his back and began to retreat towards the plains at an amiable and ambling trot.

Thus began the last phase of the celebrated Dragon of the Wilderness, which was more of a mystery than his wildest massacres and deeds of destruction. He interfered with nobody; he stood politely on one side for people to pass; he even succeeded, with some signs of reluctance, in becoming a vegetarian and subsisting entirely upon grass. But when the ultimate goal of his pilgrimage was discovered, the surprise was even more general. The wondering and still doubtful crowds that followed him across that country became gradually convinced of the incredible idea that he intended to go to church. Moreover, he approached the sacred edifice in a far more tactful and unobtrusive and respectful way than Sir Laverok had done in the old days, when he broke windows and tore up pavements in his indiscriminating excess of punctuality. Finally, the monster surprised them most of all by kneeling down and opening his mouth very wide with an ingratiating expression; and the Princess surprised them still more by walking inside.

Something in the way in which she did it revealed to the more thoughtful among them the fact that Sir Laverok had been inside the animal all the time. It is unnecessary to repeat here the explanations which gradually enlightened them about the inner truth of the story of the inner machinery of the dragon. This exact and scientific narrative is also addressed only to the thoughtful. And these will have no difficulty in guessing that a magnificent marriage ceremony took place in the interior of the dragon, which was treated as a temporary chapel while within the precincts of the consecrated building. They may even form some notion of what was meant when the Princess, who was given to oracular remarks, said, "The whole world will behave differently when heroes find their hiding-place in the world." But it must be confessed that those learned men, the Chancellor and the Chamberlain, could make very little of it.

The Second Miracle

The Missionary had wandered into a remote and savage land; around him was a wilderness of wild superstitions, of men demanding dreadful and barbaric things. Dark passions found expression in obscure rites and bewildering dances; the strange craving for erecting altars, dedicating priests and prophets, setting apart particular spaces for ceremonies connected with the supernatural, seeking divine aid in the form of a feast or a sacrifice — these and a hundred other human antics disturbed the land; and he felt an equal horror and repugnance for them all. By which it will be understood that the clergyman in question was a broad-minded clergyman, and that he belonged to the Liberal school.

In the course of his wandering he came upon a particularly flagrant case of credulity. It was a legend concerned with the hero or holy man who was said to have founded the tribe. He had been the best of men and an example to all mankind; yet (strangely enough) he had been killed. And as a mark of contempt his body was cast forth into a barren and burnt-out place of ashes and dust and dry sand, where it was notorious that nothing could grow, not even the hardiest thorn or weed. But in spite of this, said the legend, there had sprung up out of his grave in that grey desert a great green tree bearing golden fruit and flowers of all the colours in the world. The tribe sheltered under it, worshipping as in a shrine; and declared that the spirit of the dead was present in the trunk and branches. Then came an evil time of invasion; and heathens laid waste the land and cut down the tree, so that when it was recaptured by the faithful it was in the form of a mere log or lopped trunk. But they still believed that the spirit of their god was in it; and they set the sacred timber upon an altar and worshipped it, and rejoiced and prospered as of old.

The missionary really had great difficulty in explaining to these simple people their simple error. Taking a large magnifying-glass from his pocket, he examined the surface of the bark and found it to be of a ligneous nature. He had little doubt, he said, that if the timber were dissected, transverse sections and all other sections would exhibit the same tree-like formation. He even offered good-naturedly to draw up the diagrams beforehand; for he was an expert mathematician. In short, he showed that a thorough scientific analysis confirms the popular suspicion that wood is wooden. He was quite gratified with his reception; indeed, it was far better than he could have hoped. The simple savages seemed almost ready to worship him, prostrating themselves before him at a signal from the chief priest, who marched in front of him at the head of a triumphal procession, crying aloud strange words in an unknown tongue. For the Missionary did not know that the words, when translated from the hieratic tongue, were as follows: "Once more the gods are good to us! For centuries there has dwelt with us a man in the likeness of a lump of wood. And now, for a new miracle, we have a lump of wood in the likeness of a man."

The Conversion of an Anarchist

Lady Joan Garnet had eyebrows long before she had any hair; and a cock of the eyebrow from which the wisest and oldest nurses in the family deduced that she would marry the wrong man. Perhaps she did; those who read this tale must decide the point for themselves. For (however that may be) some twenty-three years afterwards, when Lady Joan had plenty of hair, almost too much in fact, and of a heavy bronze tint, she still had the distinct and defiant eyebrow, darker in colour and, as it were, disconnected from the rest of her face. But though she ran to eyebrow, she did not look supercilious; only rather cross.

She was indeed of a restless and enterprising temper, and in our modern, highly civilised society it did not take her long to find a man wrong enough to marry. The prophetic nurses, indeed, had no notion it would be as wrong as that. In the Smart Set in which she lived, men talking Socialism and Anarchism were common enough, of course, but men believing in them (or in anything else) were rare, and Andrew Home was a perfectly serious Anarchist. He was a young Scot who had worked his way up from a plough to a professorship, and been taken up by the aristocrats as aristocrats will take up anything curious — so long as it is not of ancient lineage. The rich gentleman shrinks from nobody, except the poor gentleman.

He was strong, lank, and rawboned, yet with a certain air, not uncommon in Scotch peasants, of being (in the strict and literal sense) well bred; he had a long, handsome, hatchet face with something like a sneer on it; yet he was very compassionate to the poor and to animals. He had a complete philosophic scheme of negations. He looked at Nothing from every possible point of view; he divided Nothing into sections and then recombined it into systems; he distinguished one kind of Nothing from another kind of Nothing, and then proved that the difference amounted to Nothing, after all. Yet he was not a bore, though uncontroversial persons might call him a bully; he made with Lady Joan the one mistake so often made by a clever man with a clever woman, that of arguing with her just ten minutes too long.

101

For the rest he was famous and fairly rich by this time, and when Lady Joan announced her engagement to him, the scandal that ensued did not in the least arise from his being a parvenu, still less from his being an Atheist, but solely from his refusal to be married in a church. As was pointed out by more than one member of our most intellectual class, a fellow may come from all kinds of things, and a fellow may think all kinds of things, but a fellow ought to be able to stick it out for an hour in church. The Scot was a hard man to drive; he had shaken the foundations of his fiancée's conventional morality, and his answer was a threat as well as a defiance. It amounted to a broad hint that marriage itself (if examined through his best microscope) was one of the varying and allotropic forms of Nothing, and that if they would not allow him the Registrar he would do without that official. Joan, so far from being shocked, took the thing with an innocent anarchism not uncommon in the young, and the cause of many highly intellectual elopements. In fact, she said that if she was forbidden to marry the wrong man, she would — not marry him, which would be worse. Now this is a thing still considered wrong, even by the rich.

Nevertheless, about three weeks afterwards, Mr. Andrew Home, F.R.S., was decorously and thoroughly married to Lady Joan Garnet in a fashionable church crowded with all kinds of important people with whom (Heaven be thanked) this story has nothing to do. If anyone cares to know how the conversion or surrender came about, it befell through the world-embracing beneficence of the Liberty Hall Club. Lady Joan had come in, looking particularly radiant; she was talkative and full of tales for her lover about this Bohemian (though by no means democratic) society in which she had spent an evening. "They say I may be elected to the club," she said with great relish. "But they doubt if I'm advanced enough."

"Advanced in what direction?" asked Home.

"Oh, in all directions!" cried Lady Joan, waving her muff and boa with a world-embracing gesture. "Why, that's just the point. You can say *anything* at the Liberty Hall Club — you can defend *any* view, Anarchist or Atheist or — or whatever's supposed to be worse. They include all, yes, all the opinions in the world — and then they talk."

"It must be rather stimulating for you," he said, and a shade crossed his brow that was not thought, but very ancient instinct.

"It's frightfully exciting," she agreed. "Do come with me to the meeting there this evening! You'll be sure to secure my election, and you'll probably be elected yourself. Remember," and the nature of her smile altered a little, "remember sometimes, please, that I am really very proud of you."

"All right," said Andrew Home, turning away, and putting his pipe in the rack; he also spoke in a somewhat changed voice. Two hours later they both got into a cab and drove to the place assigned.

They were received at the Club of all the opinions by a bony lady, whose green clothes clung to her like long seaweed; she had a long, wooden face, and also a long wooden arm and hand; which shot out so as to startle a guest, who could not believe an arm could be so long unless it were a telescope. To Lady Joan she said in a deep voice, "Happy to see you here again!" To Professor Home she said in a lower voice still, "We are proud of this acquisition."

The acquisition walked up the room with the heavy sneer, that was his least human trait, decidedly deepening on his face. He was in dull and strict evening dress, while the people all around him were in clothes that can be assigned to no hour of the recognised day or night: a medley of pyjamas, shooting-knickers and early morning dressing gowns might partly explain the men: a medley of winding sheets with improper bathing costumes might explain the women — only they all hastened to explain themselves. To judge by his face, the Anarchist found this explanation inadequate.

Joan knew the men she liked, as women do know men in such cases. She knew that all these men in mad costumes were harmless; and she knew that her own man was dangerous. She kept on turning her face to him to see what he thought of all the people to whom he was introduced; and each time she thought she was nearer and nearer to some lawless outbreak. She was almost relieved to think that the shabby evening clothes falling about his long, lank figure could not possibly conceal a bomb.

He was introduced to Dr. Omar Ross, an enormous atheist in almost clerical costume, above which rose a long pink neck terminating in a round, red face and a grin. He was introduced to Mr. Thaddeus Wilkes, the celebrated student of Eastern Religions; one of those unlucky little men for whom, wherever they sit, the light always catches their eyeglasses. Before the end of the evening he was actually introduced to his hostess, the lady who had welcomed him at the door. She was a Mrs. Gurge, Mr. Gurge was, presumably, out.

It may have been Joan's personal infatuation, but all these people seemed to look much smaller than they had the evening before. It seemed to her that Satan himself had come to visit a lot of little devils. She felt a disquiet and a disproportion as she heard Mr. Thaddeus Wilkes explaining to Andrew the very things Mr. Wilkes last night explained to her.

" ... every kind of opinion, you see," Mr. Wilkes was saying, "can be expressed in the club..."

"Well," said Home, with a stolid face, "suppose I express the opinion that the police ought to raid this club?"

"But you don't express that opinion," said Mr. Wilkes, cocking his eyeglasses coquettishly, "a man of your known Liberal tendencies..."

"I do express that opinion," said Home with decision. "I think everyone now in this room ought to be in jail."

"He, he; and why?" tittered the Student of Eastern Religions.

"Because we're not respectable," answered Home. "One must be respectable."

"Respectability!" shrieked the little man, leaping up and looking for his eyeglasses, "why, it's respectability that's created all the persecutions and superstitions, and abominations; all the loss of individuality, of progress, of self-ownership, and self-respect..."

"Self-respect," repeated Home, nodding. "True. And how can one respect anything that is not respectable?"

"It is a quibble — a common pun!" shrieked the eager Wilkes, but his outcry was cut through by the heavy voice of Mrs. Gurge asking, with tragic eyes on Home, the following simple question:

"Don't all these things come," she said, "because love is not free?"

"Well, of course, it isn't," said Andrew Home, simply, "love means that a man, in one respect at least, is not free."

"But would there not be more joy, more old Greek gaiety," said Mrs. Gurge in a lugubrious voice, "if marriage were abolished?"

"Why?" asked Home blankly. "The Greeks believed in marriage."

"Do you really mean to say," broke out Mrs. Gurge, with an altera-tion of voice that was as startling as an animal's cry, "do you dare to say that it's just or right that a woman should be tied to a man — that it's tolerable — that — "

"That's what I mean to say," said Mr. Home.

Then, after a pause, he added, "But I think they should be mar-ried in a church, and, therefore, of course, before three o'clock."

"And what right have you to say such things?" cried Mrs. Gurge, standing up, and trembling all over. "You are the sort that has persecuted everything — what right have you — where have you got your right?"

"I got it from you," said Home, with great gentleness. "You and this gentleman told me that all opinions are permitted in this club." He looked at the ceiling, and then proceeded, "so I think that an indissoluble church marriage, celebrated in a church before three o'clock —"

"Oh tcha!" cried Mr. Wilkes, rising with very crooked eyeglasses, "that a mere building or a mere hour can matter."

"No?" said Home, with a broad and beaming smile. "Why not?"

The little man with the eyeglasses turned with angry gestures of shoulders, but the big atheist in the semi-clerical dress bawled out in a good big parson's voice, "It's all environment."

"I beg your pardon," inquired Home brightly.

"It's all environment," bellowed the big man. "You think respec-tability's all right because you've always been respectable; you believe in being married in church because you've always been to church —"

"That must be the explanation," assented Home, getting wearily to his feet. "I always thought that perpetual church-going of mine would be my undoing. But I think, mind you," and he lifted a warn-ing finger, "I think you gravely neglect religious considerations! To say that 'it's all environment' is decidedly against sound Church teaching; it neglects the degree of self-determination evidently deducible from the dogma of original sin, as implied even in Holy Scripture and finally defined at the Third Council of Thessapol—"

"Oh, such damned rubbish," said the apoplectic Dr. Ross, and turned his back before the other could finish.

"Dr. Omar Ross, I believe?" said Andrew Home, very coolly, but in such a way as to make the big man turn his red face round again and say, "Well?"

"That man in eyeglasses," said Home quietly, "is so small that it would be smaller still to hit him. But as you are different, may I say that I am not used to these manners? I come to a club where I am expressly told that any opinion is tolerated, and while I am expressing an opinion for which thousands have died, a gentleman cuts me short in the very middle of a Greek word and turns his back on me. When that happens, there are only two other things that can happen. If we are rationalists, you will apologise. If we are savages and gentlemen, let us go and fight in the backyard."

Dr. Omar Ross gasped for a moment like a fish; his scarlet face turned a sort of salmon pink, and he answered in a quite new voice, "I will fight you if you like, but really — really! Perhaps it was rather rude of me to turn my back, but upon my blessed word, I — I'd never heard such things in my life! Sound Church teaching! And Original Sin! I do apologise, Mr. Home. I think you had a right, by the rules of the club, but really, really — there is a limit to — to —"

"There is," said Home, nodding. "There is a limit to Liberty Hall. I know now what the limit is."

Striding swiftly across the room, he reached Lady Joan, who was engaged in conversation, apparently of great gloom, with Mrs. Gurge in the doorway. As he came near he heard Mrs. Gurge saying:

"I'm very sorry, of course; extremely sorry. But I don't think I could promise anything like a chance. The vacancies in the club are so few — and — and some of the members are so very keen on having people who are really advanced, that really —"

"That really we must be going," said Mr. Home, shaking hands with her heartily. "I've never got such good out of an evening in my life. Come along, Joan; we can get a taxi at the corner."

When they had bundled into the taxi-cab, there was a long silence, and then Lady Joan said:

"You are an extraordinary person, Andrew. Are you mad?"

"Not now," he answered, with composure.

"But those people were all arguing for the things you've always been arguing for."

"Permit me a masculine distinction," said Andrew. "They were arguing badly."

"Well, you were pretty wild," she said, laughing. "And you don't believe in any of those things, respectability and marriage and all the rest that you were defending."

He was silent.

"You don't believe that a marriage must take place in a church before three; you don't believe in a church at all, and as for a Council of the Church —" And she laughed with delight.

"You have such a pretty laugh, Joan," he said very softly, "much nicer to hear than Dr. Omar Ross's."

"What *do* you mean?" she asked, and stopped, staring.

"I don't believe I can say what I mean; I don't believe you can hear it," he said, "but I have found the limit of anarchy. Anarchists will endure everything except one thing — sense. They will tolerate a hundred heresies — they will not tolerate orthodoxy. There is one thing that is sure to be right; the thing that is most hated. There is one thing that is most hated. Respectability!"

She was still looking at him with a devoted but painful curiosity; she saw his rigid face taking on that white flame which marks the eternal fanatic in every Scotchman. They are a race of the suddenly converted.

"Look at that poor chap out in the rain," he said. "That's what they call the Man of the Street. It means that he's ordinary. Why is he outcast? Because he's ordinary. He wants a house, a wife, and a baby — all the humdrum things God dreamed of when he made the world. That's why we put that man to sweep our streets and black our boots; because he wants what God wanted long ago; and not whatever we shall want the Wednesday after next. Think of him, and then think of those people in Liberty Hall Club —" A surge of disgust went over him like an earthquake — "those foxes have holes, and those vultures of the air have nests; but man has nowhere to lay his head."

"I don't think I understand it," said Lady Joan Garnet.

"Do you understand this?" asked Andrew Home. "A man will be married to a woman in a particular brick or stone church before three."

"Yes," she said. "I understand that easily."

"You were always cleverer than I," he said quite simply. "I have only just understood it myself."

Concerning Grocers as Gods

Mr. William Williams was a grocer's assistant. For many years the grocer had groced and the assistant had assisted; but of late his employer had begun to have doubts of whether he was of much assistance; and one bright and brisk spring morning he rather suddenly and dramatically ceased to assist.

As Mr. Stiggles was one of the three competing shopkeepers of a small village by the seaside, his shop had something of the general character of a village shop; and he sold several things that may or may not be defined as groceries; such as certain large vials of Home-Made Lemonade which it was William's duty at that moment to set prominently in the window. Some had been known to question some of the titles attached to the goods of Mr. Stiggles. Some had murmured that his superfine sugar had suffered contact with his sandy floor; and that his celebrated Fresh Eggs were ornaments rather of an ornathological museum than a shop. But nobody had ever disputed the title of Home-Made Lemonade; or doubted that Mr. Stiggles made it himself, by some recipe as secret as that of the Benedictine monks. Many believed sea-water to be the staple, but there was a suggestion of soap; and other ingredients such as verdigris and chopped-up grass were suspected. Mr. Stiggles came into his shop with sudden violence, to find William hurriedly concealing a cigarette; for Mr. Stiggles disapproved of smoking. It was perhaps the only suggestion of a moral sense that he ever exhibited.

"Why aren't those things in the window?" he demanded. "Pinker and Bootle have both got theirs out. Why don't you put 'em in the front where they can be seen?"

"Oh, all right," said William with a sinister air of languor. He lifted one of the large lemonade bottles and hurled it with a crash through the front window, so that it made a star of green liquid and broken glass on the cobbled street. "I should think it could be seen there," he added.

He then left the shop in a leisurely manner, and when Mr. Stiggles demanded what he was going to do, he explained.

"I'm going to pick pockets," he said. 'I'm going to live with thieves and thugs and burglars. I want a little honest company."

Mr. William Williams left his village grocer, full of a fine fury against the mean tricks of grocers in competition, but he did not have any chance of comparing their morals with those of thieves; for before he could attempt it, he met somebody who profoundly influenced his life, and gave him a larger view of thieving and other things. This was a tall man he met in a lane; a man with long wisps of hair and a wide hat; he had a very kindly and encouraging smile and bulging eyes like a mesmerist's. Perhaps he mesmerised William; anyhow he made him feel very happy and good; telling him how there was a land beyond the sea where everybody was happy and good without the least apparent trouble; for instead of two grocers fighting like cat and dog, there was one common fellowship and unity of interests between the grocer and the groced.

So William went away across the sea with the old gentleman, who was called the Prophet Hinks, and somewhere on the shining plains of America he found the shining city. It was certainly very calm and beautiful to look at, with terraces of white not divided into separate houses, but marked by doors at intervals all painted an exquisite peacock green and flanked by little shrubs in little tubs, to show that the new civilisation was not indifferent to art and beauty. But the chief thing that struck William about the new civilisation, when he came to study it, was that he could not get a cigarette there. He thought at first he might get it in the Vegetarian Hostel, as tobacco is a vegetable; but his argument was sadly waved away. He thought he might look for it in the House of Joy, otherwise called (out of William Morris) "The House of Fulfilment of Craving"; but though he had a very definite craving, he could not get it fulfilled. Then he lost his temper and said:

"If you're so fond of giving people plants in little tubs, I shall grow a tobacco-plant in my little tub.''

''*Your* little tub?'' said the Prophet Hinks in low and heart-broken tones. ''*Your* little tub? How little you have understood the spirit that is here!''

And indeed he found that Professor Hinks and his Committee were the owners of the ground as well as the buildings; and that nothing could be done that they did not want to do themselves. So he thoughtfully picked up the red Russian bowl, in which his luke-warm water had been served to him that morning, and threw that also through the window with a loud crash.

''Stiggles was a stinking rat,'' he observed. ''but at least he was only my employer and not also my landlord and my lord and my god. I'd rather go back to where they fight each other like rats, and at least show they are alive.''

So he strode away and betook himself homewards; and the nearer he came to home the more his reaction rose within him and his heart went out to the rough-and-tumble tradition of his fathers. He wanted to go back to a human place, where there was a little human and kindly hatred; where everything was not chilled and frozen with universal Love. It would be fine to see the two grocers fighting in the streets, and to take sides in the funny old family quarrels; and perhaps to find friendship and marriage as well as quarrels, and try his luck at bringing up a family and die and be buried in his own land.

When he entered his own village he stood still and stared down the principal street. There were two long perspectives of stately classical buildings, along the whole frontage of which on both sides ran an inscription in gigantic golden letters: ''Stiggles Universal Stores.'' There was no other shop or house visible in the circle of the horizon. The solid block was divided into a series of departments, flanked by little shrubs in little tubs, to show that the new system was not indifferent to art and beauty.

What struck Mr. William Williams most about the new system established by Stiggle's Stores was that he could not get a cigarette there. For Mr. Stiggles (now indeed a nobleman) retained the one moral principle in his life. He would really have felt it an unclean and unholy thing to have gained a little more money by selling the nicotian poison along with the various quack medicines, widely advertised and dangerous drugs, alcoholic cures for alcoholism and other house comforts that were provided at his Stores. But outside this honourable scruple, it really seemed that the Universal Stores was really universal, in the sense that it did really possess an inferior form of almost everything in the world. Artists might buy their colours there if they did not want the right colours; musicians might purchase violins and church organs cheaply and rapidly manufactured; indeed, people had been known to order a cathedral from Stiggles, who had put it up with the utmost rapidity, neatness and despatch. Mr. William Williams wondered whether there was something inherently wrong in his own character, whereby a strange discontent seemed still to possess him even in the most smooth and satisfactory social conditions. His mind began to revert with another unreasoning and sentimental reaction to all the real simplicity of the lunatic under the luminous American sky. They had at least in some sort of half-witted way been looking for things that are too good for this world. William was beginning in a puzzled way to tell the people in the shop about his American adventure; but when he came to mention the name of the Prophet Hinks, they were filled with horror; and the sort of pity that is akin to loathing. "He is a Socialist!" they cried, "and Socialism is fatal to individuality."

At which Mr. Williams gave a great cry, and seizing a yellow Oriental vase from the counter, he hurled it through the window with a loud crash and leapt after it, running wildly down the street and waving his arms. For he remembered that, in the days of his childhood, there had been a dark and depressing pool just beyond the bridge, which many suicides had found suitable and convenient. But in this he was intercepted; for although this enlightened community had, of course, long outgrown any prejudice against suicide, they preferred things done in a decent and orderly fashion. So he was conducted to Stiggles's Lethal Chamber in Stiggles's Death Department; and was afterwards enclosed in one of the fashionable and universally coveted Stiggles Coffins and buried in the popular and universally frequented Stiggles Cemetery. So he had his prayer, as is given to few mortals, and died and was buried in the village that was his home.

A Real Discovery
By a Would-Be Discoverer

Robert Raven was something of a mystery in more ways than one.
He was what is called a precocious child; and precocious children are
generally of two types. The more fortunate are killed; as was the Admirable Crichton at the age of twenty-two. The other sort, a doomed
and accursed race, survive; and nobody notices that they do so. But
the case of Robert Raven was rather peculiar. He had shown what
is called brilliant promise in his scientific studies at the school and
college; and what is much more important, as an indication of sinceri-
ty, he had made himself a nuisance to everybody from childhood by
surrounding himself with the litter and the stinks of very experimen-
tal chemistry. And then, quite suddenly, somewhere about the age
at which the brilliant Scot of the sixteenth century had fallen fighting
amid the Italian swords and daggers, the English infant prodigy had
retired into private life like a man of eighty.

But there was an additional mystery attaching to the case of Robert
Raven. He was comparatively poor, though he had it in his power
to become very rich, in a period when science was a fashion; and one
ordinary essential of retirement is riches, or at least a competence.
But Raven did not sink into mere poverty. On the contrary, everyone
who met him remarked that he presented a much more comfortable
figure than the lean and fanatical student who had once neglected his
meals for the sake of his experiments. It was something like the difference between the young and the old Napoleon; for there was
something Napoleonic about his eagle face and hanging hair, though
in his case the hair was red. But Napoleon looked less hungry when
he had fed upon success; and nobody had any notion of what Raven
fed on. He prospered in the shadow like some monstrous and yet
obscure vegetable growth; and among all his old scientific associates,
there was no botanist who could classify him.

It was at the period in which the new applications of physics and
electricity had reached their widest and wildest triumphs. Invisible
wires linked together the remotest continents and islands: a tangled
and tingling net of vibration and sound. Everybody travelled by

112

aeroplane, except the large but unimportant section who were too poor to travel at all; for the main lines of social distinction had of course remained untouched by scientific development. Of the more prosperous classes, who alone need concern the scientific historian, every little villa had its aeroplane shed in the garden like a dog's kennel; only the dog-kennel was often larger than the house. Every house, it need hardly be said, was fitted up with receptacles for the new signalling; and woven about with a viewless veil of voices from all the ends of the earth. American interviewers were saved the trouble of crossing the Atlantic; their flying ghosts or spirits could besiege the house and make the householder happy with their ceaseless and artless queries about all the details of the household. The less reputable member of the Smith family, who had been paid a considerable sum of money on condition of his becoming an empire-builder in the more remote parts of Canada, was enabled to revisit his home at all hours of the day; and his flowing and continuous demands for more money filled the house with the sense of something uninterrupted and familiar. The rich uncle, who was so much respected by reason of his living in Australia, was enabled to lend his somewhat loud and hearty voice to the most intimate conversation of the tea-table, as if the intervening seas and continents had been swallowed up in his large and roaring mouth, as in the mouth of Gargantua. In short, the family enjoyed all the latest comforts and conveniences that science can provide.

It was about this time that an accident led to my surprising the secret of my friend, Robert Raven. He had gone to live down in the country, as had so many other town people of his time. But unlike the other town people, he had not first deliberately gone to live in the country and then made desperate efforts to connect himself again with the town. There was no wireless apparatus on his house. There was no aeroplane-shed in his grounds. His homestead was to all appearance a survival of the quiet and isolated homesteads of the remote past; with a thatched roof and hedges that enclosed his garden like green walls. And yet it was in the very centre of this old farmhouse that I came on the discovery which revealed his hobby: the hobby which still connected him with the world of science.

It is needless to narrate here the stages of the growing suspicion that led me to the notion that my host was not always so solitary as I had supposed, in his rural solitude. I took no steps to surprise his secret; and indeed the surprise was mine, when descending to the ground floor in the middle of the night, in search of a book to beguile my sleeplessness, I found one of the flagstones of the old paved kitchen lifted like a lid and a subterranean light striking upwards from some illuminated cellar, throwing the aquiline features of my friend into an almost infernal chiaroscuro. Indeed his face and figure thus lit from below seemed for the moment so fantastic as to obliterate a less familiar presence; and it was a moment or two before I realised that he was looking down on a companion whose head appeared black and grotesque, out of the gleaming slit of the trap-door. But it was the strange man who spoke first.

"I suppose the thing will not want re-charging. It is rather difficult to come down here like this."

"It is," said Raven, with a sinister smile. "But I notice that you all manage to come."

"All!" repeated the stranger in surprise.

"You are the hundred and fifteenth this week," answered Raven.

"Why, I thought — " began the other; and then suddenly catching sight of me, ducked and disappeared.

I advanced to the edge of the hole; but could see no sign of him. I could see nothing indeed but a vast, vague pattern, as of some mazy mathematical design. The staring, unnatural light may have dazzled me; but it seemed to me that the labyrinth of lines, whatever it was, was incredibly far away; like some fallen floor of space. Raven bent over and shut the strange door; and that is all I ever saw or knew of the methods of his nameless science.

Raven stepped back to the kitchen-table and lit a candle in an old-fashioned candlestick, in quaint contrast to the dizzy and distant world of blinding illumination sealed up in the cavern below. In the more familiar light his features fell into a more natural expression; and I saw that he was smiling. He spoke in a tone of humorous resignation.

"As you've seen so much," he said, "there's no reason for not telling you the rest. There never was any reason so far as I'm concerned. It's my customers who like to keep it dark."

"Do you mean to say," I asked, "that you can live in this out-of-the-way hole and get hundreds of clients to come down to see you in your cellars; why, I never even heard of it, whatever it is that you're doing?''

"People will always come after the thing they really want," he replied. "People say the big newspapers and the advertisers are giving the public what it wants. But they aren't; they are giving the public what it doesn't want; that's why they have to push it and ram it down our throats. If the public wants something, it will run after it as it runs after me — yes, and crawl underground to get it if necessary.''

"But what is it?" I demanded impatiently. "What do you do? What have you discovered?''

"I will tell you what I do," he said, soberly. "What I do is to undo what all the other men of science are doing. It is the greatest scientific discovery of the age. That is why it is kept dark.''

"It is very dark to me," I answered. "I asked you what it is that you do?''

"And I said I would tell you," he replied. "I manufacture Distance. I manufacture Silence. All the others are making the world smaller, but I am making it larger. Don't you see that is what all these inconsistent idiots really want, when they rush deeper and deeper into the country, trailing all their telephones and telegraph wires behind them? They don't really want the roads to London made shorter. What they really want is the street in London made longer. What they want is their next-door neighbour wafted away upon a great wave of space. Nobody before me has ever manufactured space. This is the real intensive cultivation; the manufacture of small infinites. This is the real application of science to the small proprietors. This, without altering one visible boundary, gives three hundred acres to the cow.''

"And all these people who come to you," I said, "are all wanting to indulge this illusion of distance secretly, like a drug.''

"Well, it is a delicate matter sometimes, you see. To sit talking to an aristocratic but rather reminiscent maiden-aunt — or rather to sit being talked to by her — it is sometimes rather a relief to be able to make her fade gradually into the middle distance, her voice dying away like a faint farewell; but of course it is as well to conceal from her the fact that she is doing so. It could hardly be done so tactfully, if an apparatus for removing aunts were advertised on all the hoardings.''

"There certainly seems something a little cynical about it," I said. "I suppose that is why your traffic is as secret as dope."

"It has a more human side," said Raven, "though doubtless, like all scientific discoveries, it is dangerous and liable to abuse. It is a great temptation when you see somebody you do not very much like walking briskly up the road towards your house, to press a button and lengthen the road by a mile or so. To see him continuing to walk briskly forward while the road shoots telescopically backwards, to see him resuming his march with dauntless resolution and always appearing further and further away down the perspective of the street, is a gratification that many find it hard to resist. But, as I say, it has its more ideal side. It is very doubtful whether all this piling of people on top of one another, in the big cities, really leads to sympathy or social fellowship. Man is a mountain that should be seen from a greater distance. Man is a monument or a statue that requires a more open space and a simpler background. I assure you that the householder in question is often quite carried away with love and affection for the stranger, when the stranger has really become a sort of vanishing dot on the horizon. If you are English, you know that the secret of an Englishman is that he really feels sociable so long as he is in solitude."

"I must apologise for having broken into your solitude," I said, "I had really no intention of thrusting myself between you and your client."

"Not at all," replied Raven, politely. "I am sensible of no intrusion. Indeed, to tell you the truth, I have got the apparatus working now; and I have succeeded in removing you to a distance of about a mile and a half. Given these conditions, I find your company delightful."

The Paradise of Human Fishes

Mr. Peter Paul Smith had just put on a new suit of clothes; but he did not strike any special attitudes of vanity over it. His face was more or less masked with a sort of goggles, even larger than those which perfect the personal beauty of the American dude; but he was not going motoring. His trousers were as roomy and shapeless as plus fours; but he was not going golfing. His costume was in a sense a uniform, for he was an official; but it was not a uniform such as tradition associates with the ambition to fascinate the fair. It was even in a sense a bathing-suit; but not one which the most sensitive town councillor would forbid as being of a seductive indelicacy. It was in fact the costume of a deep-sea diver, with the helmet like the head of a huge owl, the four limbs like the legs of an elephant and a long pipe protruding from the back of the head like a monkey's tail in the wrong place. The town councillor might well consider the compulsory enforcement of this costume at all our watering-places, since it would at once quiet his moral alarms about mixed bathing, and extend the educational range for the innocent and scientific study of the wonders of the deep. Some such reform is bound to come sooner or later, for we live in an age of re-organised efficiency; as nobody knew better than Mr. Smith himself, who was re-organising something or other in connection with contraband; which had necessitated his going with his friend, Dr. Robinson, and a staff of assistants, who were now cautiously lowering him into the sea.

He got on much better than he had expected. Only once in the course of the first half hour's groping did he feel anything like a hitch, an instantaneous strangling sensation as if his communications were cut or caught somewhere; but it passed away; and he must have acted automatically even during the seizure, for he recovered to find himself walking stolidly on the great grey slime under the sea. At first it seemed as dark as a cavern; but he began to be conscious that the darkness itself was less and less impenetrable. The profiles of fishes seemed to be drawn in faint lines of light; as extravagant as caricatures of politicians. It was as if devils as well as angels could have halos. But the

halo came from a faintly increasing light which turned the twilight
at last into a transparency unnatural in colour but luminous enough
as a medium for movement. Smith thought of a great green sunrise.
It suggested some grand savage myth about the sun being drowned
in the sea. He was surprised, however, to find how soon he grew accustomed to the green daylight. Something in the elemental transi-
tion had acted like the transit of time; he felt as if he had been walking on that slimy floor for a hundred years. The smooth and serpen-
tine columns of titanic seaweed seemed to him quite as natural as trees;
tall trees round which the birds dart and wheel. For an instant he
almost expected the birds to sing; when he remembered that they were
fishes; the dumb birds of those buried skies.

He stood still and stared at something in front of him. The shapeless
slime rose into the shape of a sharp ridge with an opening cut through
it, cut sharply and squarely as by the hand of man. Through this opening gleamed stripes and patches of all the colours of sunset, as when
one looks through a gate into a garden. It was a garden; and none
the less a garden because a glimpse of hundreds of writhing tentacles
or twiddling fingers showed that it was made of sea anemones instead
of flowers. They were arranged in mathematical patterns following
their variegated colours, as nature does not arrange them. At the end
of the straight path between the coloured plots was the low dome of
a building, dark against the light of whatever mysterious dayspring
illumined those springs of the sea. Grey gleams clinging to it here
and there suggested some metal like lead or pewter. It might have
been a giant diver's helmet; and coming towards him down the path
surmounted by the dark streak of his pipe of communication was
another diver. But as the man came nearer, he saw that the helmet
was of another shape than his own, moulded into other metal features,
like those of a mask. He had a momentary thrill at the thought that
the head inside the helmet might also be of a strange shape; that the
thing looking at him out of its windows was not a man.

On this, however, he was soon reassured. The stranger unhooked
some apparatus resembling a telephone and clapped it against Smith's
helmet; he immediately felt a new electric throbbing, and then the
unmistakeable voice of the United States speaking very distantly in
his ear.

"See here," said the voice, "has the City Inspector seen you?"

"What Inspector? What City?" asked Smith.

"Why, our City, of course. Gubbina City," answered the native.

"Good heavens," cried Smith. "You don't mean to tell me that men actually *live* down here."

"Only seventy-five thousand of them at present," admitted the other man, "but we're an expansive burg. You must be about the only guy that don't know how Old Man Gubbins bought all the bottom of the Atlantic dirt cheap, because all the other boobs thought it was only dirt with nothing to it. He's planted his factories here; and I tell you, Sir, this is going to be the new civilisation. Folks used to put paradise above the sky, but I guess the real paradise is going to be under the sea."

"It's got a garden like paradise anyhow," said Smith, "a garden of sea-anemones for flowers. You'll be telling me next you have a dogfish chained up instead of a dog."

"Why, as to that," answered the other, "these private fancies aren't exactly encouraged by the old man, and he says the gardens have got to go. Of course in our situation we have to do pretty much as we're told by the headquarters on land; and the old man likes to keep his finger on the string — I guess we're all on a string; and if we did have a dog, it would be on a chain."

"And I think you're on a chain yourself," said Smith. "What an awful life — to live and die breathing air that is only pumped down to you by the favour of somebody miles away."

"Where do you live?" asked the American abruptly.

"Brompton," replied Smith; he found the conversation had become quite easy, easier than an ordinary telephone.

"Are there many brooks in Brompton?" asked his companion, "or have you a well in your front garden, or do you go out and drink the rain? No, you have all your water pumped to you by the favour of somebody miles away. I don't see there's much difference between us. You are surrounded by air and have water pumped to you. We are surrounded by water and have air pumped to us. But we should both die if anything went wrong."

"You must have great confidence in Mr. Gubbins and the people who sent you down," said Smith. "Suppose he sold the plant to somebody else; suppose he went mad; suppose there was a strike or a revolution. Who are these gods who sit above you in the heights and give you the very breath of life in your underworld?"

"Let's see," said the other, with an air of abstraction, "I forget the names of the Water Board that supplies Brompton."

"My God," cried Smith, "and I never knew them either!"

Then he was silent and stared away into the distance beyond the dome. He saw something that looked at first like a forest of very thin trees of almost infinite height; then he saw it was a bunch or fringe formed of countless filaments like the filament he had seen attached to the distant figure of the other diver. It seemed to waver in a rhythmic manner and then gradually recede.

"Men falling in for work," said his informant briefly.

"It's horrible," cried Smith suddenly. "They are like marionettes."

"I fancy you people are hung on wires too; telephone wires; telegraph wires; all sorts of wires. But it's odd you should mention marionettes; for there really is a proposal for something of the sort. Some of them up there think the work could be better checked if wires were really attached to the arms and legs of the operatives, so that — what are you doing?"

"I'm going back!" cried Smith, "I'm going back where I can get a breath of fresh air."

"No," said the other, and his voice rang sad and hollow in his helmet. "That is the one thing you can never do. You cannot go back. You cannot go back to the primitive man drinking of the river. This is the way the whole world is going; if you did return to your own cities, you would soon find them so thick with chemical vapours that air will have to be pumped into them from the country outside. But you will never go."

He lurched forward and caught the other diver by his vital part, which is the pipe above him, only to be caught by the other in the same fashion. They hung there in a deadlock, each in a new fashion with his grip on the other's wind-pipe. Then Smith felt everything blacken about him, and awoke very slowly to find Dr. Robinson administering first aid on the pier.

"You're all right," he was saying, reassuringly, "You weren't down ten minutes when the thing caught somehow for a jiffy — here, you needn't be so energetic as that yet. Where do you think you're going?"

"Brompton," replied Smith, rising on wavering legs, "I want to see if anything — if anything more's happened there."

The Great Amalgamation

(From the lost Book of Arthur, mentioned by Geoffrey of Monmouth.)

...But when Sir Percivale, the good knight, came to the mouth of the mighty cavern where the monster lay, he was sore astonished to behold the heaps of whitened bones of them that had gone before him on the quest, with here and there the cloven shield or splintered lance of some knight who would ride no more. And there went to and fro amid the mounds of death an aged man with a grey beard, that was a wizard, and seemed to be numbering the bones and writing down the names of the dead in a great book.

"By my science," he said, "I am thus enabled to prophesy what are the chances of any champion's good fortune. For the laws of number cannot lie; and it is my pleasure, fair sir, to bid you know that there are now five thousand three hundred and seventy-two chances to one, that the end of your venture will be evil."

But Sir Percivale, being young and careless of science, hardly heard the words of the wise man; but rather lamented aloud over the dead, among whom lay many whose crests and quarterings he knew; and cried weeping:

"Alas, Sir Fortinbras, the good lord, that was clad from head to heel in copper and red gold and his hair red as a sunset; like a fire or a moving furnace was he ever in the front of battle; and here he lies pale like ashes. And woe is me for the good knight Sir Scudemore that dwelt in the high wood and drew the bow of which the shafts were like thunderbolts; six heathen kings they slew in the path that went down to Severne.

And while the young man wept, the old man smiled and said, as one who speaks comfortably to another:—

"Trust me, Sir Knight, that all is well with them; and that they have but amended the folly of their first attempt. For it was their error that they went always one by one, so that the foe could devour them piece-meal; but now they have become part of a mighty order and act together always, without it being possible for one to go lonely or to stray; fierce and smiling youth at which the sun stands amazed; and when that might and splendour comes out of its cavern, it is as though there were a new sunrise at moon.''

And even as he spoke, there was a far-off movement as if in dim and distant halls hollowed out of the very heart of the mountains; and along vast and vaulted corridors there was a trampling as of many terrible feet and a high hard noise like the trumpets before an army; and a moment after there came out into the sun a vast and fearful thing, covered with scales larger than scutcheons, and rayed with spikes standing out like many spears; carrying with it all the weapons of an army and yet one soul and one body, such as God permits to walk upon the hills of the world. For this was the Dragon, that had devoured many men, and Sir Percivale spurned aside the sage and the scattered bones, and, with a great cry, set his lance in rest...

On Secular Education

Once upon a time a boy was born in a square enclosure between four blank walls, where he grew up without knowledge of any other place; nor did he remember his mother or what had become of her. The only person he ever saw, as he grew up, was a sort of Guardian or Warder of the place, who passed a great deal of the time walking round and round the top of the walls like a sentinel. He was a rather remarkable old party, with a quaint sort of old-fashioned top hat and very big and bushy beard or whiskers. But he wore a very big and powerful pair of spectacles, which showed that he was delightfully scientific as well as nearly blind; and he always carried under his arm a big gun; which was enough to prove that he was the Law and the Executive.

The occupation of the boy, to which he was introduced very early in life, was as follows. In one of the walls there was a round hole, just large enough to allow a sort of iron rope or rod to pass out across the enclosure and vanish into an exactly identical round hole in the opposite wall. In this continuously moving cord it was the boy's business to cut notches at very exact intervals and with very considerable exertion. Sometimes, at noon and late at night, he was allowed to desist, to sleep and eat a little food which the old gentleman brought to him; and on these occasions the old gentleman was so kind as to utter a short homily of the most humane and sympathetic sort; pointing out the privileges which the youth enjoyed in so orderly and reliable an environment.

"You have complete liberty of thought," explained the Guardian, "and you are doubtless exercising that faculty by admiring the neatness of the mechanism and wondering how less happy human beings can support a rude existence without it."

"Well," answered the boy, "it must be remembered that I have never yet seen any other human beings, happy or otherwise. As a matter of fact, I am rather wondering who I am."

"We will resume this discussion in twelve hours' time," said the Guardian, looking at his watch, "when the conversation will turn upon what is the most hygienic meal-time."

The youth resumed his labours; but his mind was clearly given over to a morbid brooding, for he actually stopped in the middle of his pleasing industry to say:

"What is all this for?"

"Enjoying as you do complete liberty of speech," replied the old gentleman on the wall, "you will probably wish to discuss whether your hour of sleep should be fifteen minutes later."

"I mean," cried the boy, with a gesture as of despair, "where does all this stuff go to?"

"The complete liberty of public discussion of which you justly boast," remarked the Guardian, "will be resumed in three weeks' time."

So the boy took up his chopper again and began to chop bits out of the iron rope until he was weary; when he suddenly hurled his chopper over the wall and flung out his arms with a wild gesture to the sky.

"Who made all this?" he cried, "Who built this place, and why?"

"Silence!" cried the Guardian from the wall, in a voice of thunder, "You enjoy complete liberty of thought and speech; and I will not allow you to be fettered by Creed or Dogma."

A Fish Story

There was a thoughtful silence in the inn parlour, when the fisherman had finished a statement accompanied with wide lateral gestures but exact calculations. The parson said in a ruminant manner:

"They say the first story about a fish was the story of Jonah."

"What do you mean?" said the fisherman indignantly, "are you implying that you don't believe my story?"

"It is far more improper," said the parson, controlling the corners of his mouth, "for you to be implying that I don't believe the story of Jonah."

"Why, nobody believes that nowadays," snorted the fisherman, "science exploded all those fairy tales long ago. Even you parsons can't explain how a whale could swallow a man."

"There are things almost as hard to swallow," observed his clerical companion. "For that matter, science itself has her fish stories. Look at Wells's scientific romances; and some that have come true as well."

"That's just the difference," replied the angler excitedly "those can be explained; you may not know the explanation but a scientist could explain them step by step. The mind of man is the explanation; I can always believe that a man can do marvellous things."

"Evidently," said the parson gravely.

"Yes," interposed the traveller, who had so far remained silent; for he was a stranger in these parts and not a country gentleman like the fisherman; he was (I am sorry to say) a journalist; and on a walking tour at that. None the less he continued, though in a low and almost hollow voice, "yes, it's the human explanation that counts. I remember a trifling incident that happened to me when I was young; which shows how a little human ingenuity will produce something that seems quite odd for the moment. I used to fish as a boy, as boys do, with any bit of string or bent pin that came to hand; I had a good deal of luck; and I have prided myself since on getting practical results without bothering much about theory or expert advice. I think I was a bit put off all that by an old uncle of mine, who was so fearfully theoretical that he would go and study the skeletons of fishes in the museum, and pore over diagrams and sections of the cells and organs of fishes, before he would even go out to catch a tittlebat in a pond. The consequence was that the poor old boy got his legs entangled in his own tackle the first time he ever went fishing and fell off the end of a pier and got drowned, just when he was explaining the system of nerve-centres in some of the polyps of the South Seas. Well, as I say, I think this old tragedy of my Uncle William drove me to the opposite extreme: but I went about whipping all the streams and seas of the world with anything that came handy, and swearing that experience is the only way to anywhere. Sometimes I used the wrong thing and caught a log; sometimes, by some mistake or other, I used the right and caught nothing. They say any stick is good enough to beat a dog with; any rod is good enough to catch a shark with — that was my motto and a very good one, even if it didn't catch the shark. It caught other things, of course. As the other proverb says, anything was fish that came to my net; and when I had played an old hat for hours at Margate and nearly been pulled into the water by a plunging packing case bent on escape, I told myself that I was getting experience every hour.

"One evening about dusk I was sitting near the end of a long, narrow stone breakwater that ran out into a gently troubled sea. The waves swayed and swelled restlessly but with little noise, now and again rising high enough before they sank to catch a gleam from the last livid strip of sunset. Then, as I watched through the growing twilight such surges rise and fall, I became conscious of one that rose and did not fall. The ridge of the high wave remained rigid against the sky as if suddenly frozen into an iceberg; then I looked again and myself seemed turned to ice. The black shape was the shape of a fin, like the fin of a shark, but as big as the flapper of a whale. The next moment the world turned upside down.

"I might have thought it was an earthquake, or rather a seaquake; for a mountain had risen out of the sea. Only I saw that the mountain had eyes; eyes as huge as bay windows and standing out of its head almost like horns. The monster was of a dim purple shade changing below to a chocolate or dark red fringed with fins lined as with copper or red gold. But I had but an instant to observe it, for by the next it had butted into the breakwater shaking it from end to end like a vibrant cord; and in that same instant I knew the monster had my hook in its mouth. And then something happened that convinced me I was not awake: or there was no reason in Nature. What followed was nightmare enough, but nothing could ever equal that first departure from the sanity of sight. Instead of rebounding from the breakwater or breaking it, the great fish threw one fin across it, seeming to clutch as with a claw. Then with one huge, sickening heave, it heaved itself on to that wall of stone and remained balanced on it, like a balloon on a tightrope, its fins waving on each side to keep the balance like the wings of an enormous bird. In desperation, I plucked at my line, only to find it pulled in the opposite direction and myself along with it. The thing did not move; but by some munching or swallowing motion it was sucking my line into its inside as a windlass winds up a rope. I was dragged to its very jaws before I had time to let go. Then line and rod vanished with a flick and a jerk down the living cavern, and I turned and ran back along the causeway, shrieking aloud. Once I looked wildy over my shoulder, and beheld a new horror. The monster had moved. It was measurably nearer to me than it had been. How in the name of Hell a fish could thus live and walk out of water I did not know; but I knew I was being pursued with a mysterious malignity; it was like being hunted by a giant snail. When I came to the steep slopes of grey, glimmering, multitudinous pebbles, they sank and failed under my feet, even as all reality was failing under me. It was like trying to escape on a treadmill. I tumbled on my face, as if to bury my head in the heaped-up stones in despair; and I heard behind the dragging and shifting noises of the shingle, as the shapeless fish crawled up the hill; the land of the living, where it had no right to be alive. Then I turned recklessly and realised, as a final light of unreason, that it was dead. It was moving: but it was dead. It was marching inland on its flat fins like a huge starfish; but it was dead. Something told me there was no light behind those protuberant eyes that glistened in the growing moonshine; and in a final fury, I caught up a spar of sea-timber that lay on the shore and struck furiously at the foe. The spar had a long, rusty nail standing out like the head of a pickaxe. It rent the monstrous bulk from end to end, like the ripping up of a balloon; and from the inside there stepped out my Uncle William, whom I had not met for years.

"After the usual family greetings and inquiries, he explained everything in a quite satisfactory and entirely scientific manner. The whole story, indeed, is a most profitable lesson to the young, showing that diligence and study are always profitable in later life. Those scientific researches, which I had thought so abstract and theoretical, were not thrown away. We all are scientific enough to know the thing as a general theory; we know that touching particular nerves produces reflex actions jerking particular limbs. But as but few of us have ever happened to be swallowed alive by an enormous prehistoric fish cast up out of the deep seas by a submarine volcano, we have had but little opportunity of seeing the problem, so to speak, from the inside. My Uncle William, with his immense knowledge of ichthyology, and especially of anatomy and nerve structure, soon found that it was possible to work the fish from the inside, just as if he were steering a boat. The interior of a prehistoric fish is a simple and unpretentious place; and he was as well acquainted with the points at which it communicated with motor nerves and muscular action as you are with the corners of your room containing the telephone or the electric bell. He was thus enabled, long after the fish was dead, to travel about in it, visiting foreign countries at leisure, and even forcing the fish to perform many athletic acts to which it was quite unaccustomed in life. Such are the profoundly practical advantages of purely theoretical study."

The traveller looked around him with an air of simple benevolence; then he seemed to remember the argument, and turned to the parson with a polite explanatory gesture.

"Now why can we all believe a story of that simple sort immediately?" he asked. "Why is it instantly accepted by all as reasonable, and even probable, in itself? Why do none of you feel any of that faint scepticism about my story which distresses you in the Biblical story? Because there is nothing supernatural about it. It needs nothing beyond man as our friend says, the mind of man is the explanation and the scientist can explain it step by step. It is plainly preposterous to say that God who made the fishes could open and shut a fish's mouth if He liked. But we can believe anything, as our friend says, about the marvellous things that Man can do. That is why my story, so to speak, carries conviction on the face of it."

"I'm hanged if I know what you mean," grumbled the fisherman. "Are you making fun of the parson?"

"That must be it, I think," said the parson, cheerfully putting his pipe in his pocket, and he smiled at the traveller; and they parted.

On Private Property

When Captain Nicholas Nicholson found himself falling head downwards through empty space, the whole of his previous life passed before him. At least if it did not, the narrator of his adventures will certainly say it did; as it affords that unscrupulous scribe the most rapid method of describing who the Captain was and how he happened to be in mid air at the moment. He would describe at some length the life at a public school, the first faint stirring of the human brain at Cambridge, the joining of a Socialist society, the growing belief in social order and system of the German type so abruptly interrupted by enlistment in 1914, the incident of the girl in the tea-shop of whom he could never find further traces, the quarrel with the solicitor who had put all the family patrimony to the higher purposes of finance, and finally the experiences in the Air Force which had terminated in the way described above.

He never heard himself crash; but he came to semi-consciousness in an atmosphere of racking clamour which gradually lessened till he heard voices round him; one saying something about somebody having an artificial leg and the other observing that such legs were very beautifully made nowadays. Then he relapsed into unconsciousness with an under current of pain; and woke in a white light to see men standing about in white clothes and wearing spectacles; he supposed they were Prussians, but their faces looked hard and alien enough to be Chinese. The talk was still of the excellence of artificial limbs; and looking down, Nicholas saw that his own legs had been replaced by lengths of shining steel rods with mechanical joints of glittering complexity.

"Well," he said, forcing his courage to cheerfulness, "by your account it is almost as good as having real ones."

"It is much better," said a man with shaven head and shining spectacles, without a movement in his wooden face, "The leg of nature is a most inefficient instrument."

"Come now," said Nicholas, "if that were true you might just as well cut off my arms as well."

"We are going to," said the man in goggles.

Darkness redescended and when he awoke he was sitting up with metal arms and legs and looking down a long white-washed corridor; and the man at his side told him breakfast would be ready in half-an-hour. They walked past rows of doors, as in the passages of an hotel, and outside each door stood a pair of steel legs, newly burnished, like the boots left outside bedrooms to be cleaned.

"You won't want your legs at breakfast," said his companion; and such was clearly the case; for he was lowered by a sort of chain from above so that his truncated body fitted into a hole in the long benches flanking the tables. He had left his legs in a sort of cloakroom, duly receiving a ticket. He said something about exercise; and was gravely told that after the meal (which was of a simple but scientific sort) he would parade for a proper constitutional in the grounds. It is true that when the time came for this, he was in turn relieved of his arms, by another official (duly receiving a ticket for them) since science had already discovered that arms are not used in walking or legs in eating.

After this his story becomes a little confused; there are improbable passages about his renewing the quarrel with the solicitor and sending for legs to kick him, or reunion with the tea-shop girl and a temporary lack of arms with which to embrace her; but familiar faces and old emotions often come back in this confused way in dreams; and this experience must be regarded as a dream; for he shortly woke up in an ordinary hospital and found the world had not yet progressed quite so far as he had fancied.

The End of Wisdom

We have all had dreams or memories about some gang of pirates, grim to the point of the grotesque, as they were in the story-books of childhood, who yet pointed with awe, and almost with horror, at some super-pirate in the background; a solitary and sinister figure, compared with whose unsearchable wickedness they were all as innocent as an infant school. Such was the attitude of the hard-headed and acquisitive business men of Bison City, Ill., U.S.A., towards a certain Mr. Crake, who had committed the Unpardonable Sin.

He committed it at a lucheon party of the B.B.B., supposed by some to stand for "Better and Brighter Bisons," but by the moderate for "Better and Brighter Business." The room in the large hotel was already decorated with American flags and also with bright bunches of American ladies, the beauty and fashion of Bison City, who were allowed to lean over the stone balustrade of the gallery and look down on the Bisons feeding. But the Bisons themselves were rather late, as is the habit of the brisk business-like salesmen of those parts; and for some time there was only one lean, leathery, bilious-looking man, whose profound gloom was relieved by a large disc or label on his coat, inscribed, "Call me Johnny." After a time, however, similar revellers arrived with similar decorations; notably a white-haired withered little man, whose label bore the blazon of, "Please, I'm Tom," and a very hearty, heavy man, with dark sleek hair, whose disc was adorned with the words, "Oh, Boy, I'm Little Frankie." As the seats gradually filled up, it was seen that all the guests were decked with such gay proclamations, except two. One of these was evidently a guest of importance from outside: a compact, carefully dressed man, with yellow hair, which shone like yellow soap. The other sat further down the table, dark and angular, with a hatchet face, which was somehow handsome, and a rather sullen expression. This was John P. Crake; but there was no invitation, either in his dress or in his demeanour, to call him Johnny.

He was far from being an outcast, however; his fellow-townsmen being only too delighted to recite the precise number of dollars which he made every week in the biggest business in that neighbourhood. For Americans, who are accused of loving money, have this most generous trait: that they can actually love each other's money. They were ready to put it down to his being "sick," in the American sense, if he really failed to rejoice in the eloquence around him. That anybody could be sick of it, in the English sense, never crossed their minds. He heard the big dark Bison still orating: ". . .A man like that's just God's own American citizen and won't stay down. He goes right out for the highest ideal in sight. He won't stay 'put' with ten thousand dollars when there's twenty thousand dollars knocking around. Now we figure that about the highest ideal going is this Service. . . ." As in a dream, Crake heard the voice change, and knew that the yellow-haired politician was speaking: ". . . Here on false pretences, gentlemen. I am not a Bison. Nor was George Washington, but he would have been. (Cheers.) Wasn't it just this ideal of Service. . . ." There were more cheers, silence, a little commotion, and Crake heard his own name. Everybody was looking at him; they wanted a speech; a speech from the first citizen of Bison City. He refused. They cheered and hammered the table as if he had accepted. He refused again. The man from Washington, shining all over with diplomacy and yellow soap, insinuated his persuasion; could not be expected to leave Bison City without hearing its greatest American citizen. John P. Crake boiled with black indescribable rage and shot suddenly and rigidly to his feet. He began in a harsh jarring voice:

"Gentlemen. We're all here to tell lies, and I'll begin with that one. Gentlemen." He gazed around at the somewhat startled audience and went on: "We all tell lies in business, because we only want to make money; but I can't see why the hell we should tell lies for fun in the lunch hour. I don't care a blasted button for Service, and I don't intend to be anybody's servant; certainly not yours. Every business man here wants to make money for himself, including me; and though he may use other men, he doesn't care if they're dead and damned when he's used them. That's the reality, and I like doing business with realities. As for ideals, I've nothing to say of them except that they make me sick as a dog." He sat down more slowly and with a greater air of calm and relief.

It would be hard to say how the luncheon party broke up; but the first to come was the last to go. For, as Crake went out of the room, he found the lean bilious man looking more unpleasant than ever, because his face was deformed with a smile.

"Good for you," he said, showing his yellow teeth. "I daren't do it; I have to wear this fool thing. But that's the way to get on top. Treat 'em like dirt." After pause, he added: "Say can I see you about that consignment?"

"Come round to my office at four," said Crake abstractedly, and went out.

At four he was going through a pile of letters, not without a grim smile. Personal letters had already begun to arrive, sent round by hand as a sequel to his disgraceful outburst. Ladies especially, whom he had never seen in his life, remonstrated with him at enormous length over his unfamiliarity with Ideals. Some recommended particular books, especially their own books; some particular ministers, at whose feet a taste for ideals might be imbibed. As he turned them over, the bilious man was shown in, a certain J. Jackson Drill, a broker, and, incidentally, a bootlegger. Crake pushed the papers across to him with a gesture of contempt; a contempt, it is to be feared, which included Mr. Drill as well as the papers. For Crake was inconsistent, like many such men; and did not really like the dirty pessimism of Jackson Drill any more than the greasy optimism of Little Frankie. Perhaps the cynic does not respect somebody else's cynicism.

Drill picked up the letters with his unpleasing grin, and began reading fragments aloud:" ... If your ideals do not satisfy you, I am sure you have not heard the real message of the Broad Daylight Church, which promises spiritual progress and business success for all. The Church is now in serious need of funds. ..." Drill dropped the letter and took up another: "...May a sister in the sight of God express her grief at the dreadful avowal revealing your spiritual state touching dollars. Wealth is worthless in itself (seem to be a lot of Bible references here; handwriting very illiterate); it is a means to an end, and some of our wealthiest citizens set a noble example. ..." Drill picked up a third letter, remarking, "Not so illiterate; nice handwriting," but continued in the same derisive sing-song, "I have been thinking about what you said today, and I cannot decide whether it was the Only Way. Of course, I see your point. If these people go on being idealists, there won't be a decent ideal, or a decent idea left in the world. Somebody must do something to stop their befouling everything. Courage has come to mean readiness to risk other people's money. Service has come to mean servility to any rich man who waddles along."

Crake had lifted his head and was listening, suddenly alert with curiosity, but the other went droning on:

"Somebody must do something; and you did do something. You broke the back of it with sheer brutality; but I can't help wondering whether there isn't another way. I expect you've wondered yourself; because you are not a brute. You're supposed to be sulky because you are always longing for a little time to yourself, to think these things out. So am I."

"Here," said Crake sharply, "give me that letter."

"Rather a scream, isn't it?" said Drill; "it goes on, 'If we can't shut off this deafening nonsense, we shall have no inner life at all....' "

Crake snatched the letter out of his companion's hand with a violence that tore it across at the corner. Then he spread it out before him and looked at Drill; and Drill knew that he was not wanted in that room any more.

The letter was an extraordinary letter. The extracts he had heard gave no real idea of it. There were moments when he thought he was reading his own diary. In some cases it was rather as if he were looking into his own subconsciousness. It was signed with an evasive female pen-name, and had an address that was no clue to identity. Yet he was not primarily impressed with how much, or rather how little, he knew about the writer. He was impressed with how much the writer knew about him. She knew one thing at least, which he hardly knew himself till he had done reading. That he hated ideals and idealism because he was himself very much too bitter and fastidious an idealist. That he hated his wealth and his work and his fellow-workmen because of an unnamed comparison and because his kingdom was not of this world. He sat down and wrote a long and even laborious letter in reply; the beginning of a prolonged private correspondence that spread over years. And through all those years he never made an effort (so strong was something in him making for refinement and renunciation) to find out the name or dwelling of the woman who was his best friend.

For some little time Bison City did regard Mr. Crake as something between a leper, a lunatic, a wicked wizard commanding the elements and the blasphemer whose duty it is to be struck by lightning in the religious tracts of that region. Americans do not worship riches in the sense of forgiving anything to the rich; and they do not easily forgive a blasphemy against the gods whom they do worship. Mr. Crake had defied the gods of the tribe that were of stone and brass— especially brass. He had violated the highest morality of Bison City, which is well named, because its morality consists of going at anything with your head down. Yet, strangely enough, Mr. Crake grew happier as time went on, and even more good humoured with his fellows; so that his unpopularity began to fade away. In fact, his loneliness was ended. He no longer boiled with an incommunicable disgust. He poured out his feelings every night in long letters to his unknown friend; and received letters which had a slow but steady effect of restoring him to sanity and even to sociability. In this respect his invisible companion both puzzled and pleased him. She had read much more than he, though he was not an uncultivated man; but she seemed to have reached a balance from the study of opposite extremes. Left alone, with one book at a time, he might have been tempted to go mad like Nietzsche or turn peasant like Tolstoy. But she seemed to have accepted all the abnormalities and then returned to the normal. She was sufficiently cultured to know even the case against culture; and he could not shock her by cursing books as he shocked Bison City by cursing business. The result was that, unknown to himself and by minute gradations, he was turning from a monomaniac into a man. And then, one fine day, something happened to him, that suddenly revealed to him his manhood; which came on him with a rush like a return of boyhood.

And the strangest thing about it was this: That when he sat down, on the evening of that fine day, to write the letter that had become like a diary, to be read only by a second self, he found for the first time that he could not write. At least it seemed in a new unnatural way impossible...almost indecent. Nothing might seem more remote than that relation; yet his friend had always remained a woman; the mere fact, the slope of the feminine handwriting, a hundred delicate details, had left hanging over the affair that distant and disembodied sentiment that can never be conjured away; something like the smell of old gardens or that dust of dead roses that was preserved in old bowls and cabinets. He knew now that he had been living through a long convalescence in the large rooms of some such ancient and quiet house; under the large tact of an invisible hostess. And what had just happened to him, in the street outside, was so vivid and violent, so concrete, so incongruous. After poising his pen for a moment of doubt, he dismissed the matter, and only answered her remarks about the poetry of Claudel. And then a strange thing happened; giving him a rather terrifying sense of being watched in that house of healing by an all-seeing eye. For she wrote, in her next letter, quite casually and even humorously: "Something has happened to you. I was very much interested in what you did not tell me."

Then he told her; but it was an effort, and he felt for the first time that he was living in two worlds. As he walked where the town opened into a country road, he had suddenly realised that he was happy. His cure was complete. The disease of disdain for common things no longer devoured his brain, and yet his appreciation of the common was no nearer to the vulgar. Indeed, the common things around him, the stones in the road, the weeds in the ditch, stood out with a distinctness that was the reverse of flat. It was as if he had felt the third dimension for the first time. It reminded him of something his friend has said about religion, as compared with the mere herding both of Capitalism and Communism. "There is a delicacy about the Day of Judgment." It was at least supposed to deal with individuals. "Yes, that is it," he said to himself. "They used to say in the sight of God we are all distinguished. We may be damned; but, damn it all, we're distinguished."

He was wandering away into the nondescript landscape outside the wooden town, dotted with frame-houses and the thin trees of those plains, now lit up with the delicate clarity of the Indian summer. A born critic, born in a world where criticism is rare, he had often felt something frail and collapsible about the frame-houses of his country; as if they would fold up flat like a portable stage; something of the nomadism of a travelling show. But in his new normal mood it pleased him—not so much that they should shut as that they could open—as a child is pleased when a hinged toy opens like a telescope. Then something happened which showed sharply how very new was the mood, and even how very abnormal was the normality. He caught sight of a string stretched across a backyard, with some coloured clothes hanging on it; some of them seemed to be blouses or pinafores such as artists wear; some pyjamas of a garish cut and pattern. Before he had begun to browse in that great library of his literary correspondence, he would have felt the sight as the most unsightly sort of commonplace. A woman hanging out the washing would have been something on a level with the Comic Strip in the loathsome local paper. But at this queer moment of his life he actually liked it. The headless figures of the shirts, the dancing legs of the pantaloons looked like giant marionettes acting a pantomime in the sunlight of Italy; the stripes and patches of crude colour had the note of carnival. He thought inconsequently of the double fate of the word "Pantaloon." A very strenuous young woman was struggling with the line; and her copper hair in the sun gave a touch that brought to life the colours of a blue and green frock fluttering behind her. The garments on the line were puffed out by the wind into preposterous shapes of hollow solidity; and just at that moment a very big one, looking like a complete suit of yellow, broke from its peg and went careering across the bushes towards him, like some fat yellow buffoon dancing across the countryside. He made one wild leap and caught the runaway, which collapsed like a balloon and then hung like a rag; and, bounding across the grass plots and pathways, solemnly handed it to the young woman, who was already laughing.

"Oh, thank you very much," she said, "that's Uncle Bill. He's supposed to be an artist and likes yellow. Used to have to do with something called the Yellow Book."

"The Yellow Peril, I should think," said Crake, "but artists are proverbially liable to abscond."

"So all my business uncles tell me," she said. "I'm afraid I don't understand either sort. They would never condescend to run after the washing."

"I wish they ran after anything so clean," replied Crake. "In the business and politics I've seen—Well, there isn't any washing, only whitewashing."

She was looking at him in an unembarrassed manner, slightly amused; she had a square, open face which would have been even conventionally handsome if her wide, blue eyes had not been a shade too far apart; everything else about her expressed only the strength and strenuous bodily vigour of her first attitude; and she had one trick that is only found in people who are physically almost perfect. When she was not darting and dashing about she stood absolutely still.

His eyes strayed towards the little wooden house to which the yard was attached; and she answered his unspoken question without losing her steady smile.

"No, I'm not the Hired Help; I rather doubt if I'm a Help at all. But the rest of the family's out."

"Ah, of course," he said, "the yellow gentleman is your uncle."

"The Scarlet Woman is my aunt," she said, indicating another garment. "She has gone to hear a Hindoo who lectures on Health-Spirals and the Super-Gland."

"I know him," said Crake gloomily, "he deepens your inner life and gives you tips about Wall Street."

"The peacock blue and green contraption is my sister," she went on. "She's gone to the Purple Possum, the celebrated playground of the New Youth. All very brilliant, I believe, and prides itself especially on being Frank. What did you say?"

"Oh, nothing," said Crake, who had involuntarily murmured, "Oh, boy, I'm Little Frankie."

"Uncle goes to a speakeasy; but it's supposed to be one for artists. It's all too intellectual for me. Will you come inside?"

"Intellectuals haven't intellect enough to boil an egg," he said as he went inside. "I'm all for the eggs."

And as he went in through the sheds and sculleries and kitchen, bowing his head a little, something was whispering in his ear: "You will not return; you will not come back free; you are going into a new world; a little, real world. You are going to live in a dolls' house; and you will come out a doll."

And the change that was already in his heart made him answer with a challenge: "What a fool Ibsen was," he muttered. "What could be jollier than living in a dolls' house?"

And when he went through the dark interior and saw at last the light from the front windows, it was not the dead daylight he had left behind; for those windows looked on to the strange streets of some other star; he was in love.

A few days afterwards, with his head full of these new things, that capered in many colours like the headless puppets in the sun, he came back suddenly into the cool shadow of that older friendship in which he had lived so long. He opened the letter, which went straight to the point, silently and from within, as was her strange habit.

"You understood my first letter at once; when most men would have thought I was mad. You will understand that this is my last letter quite as easily. You will not think any of the vulgar things: jealousy or the fear that somebody else will be jealous. You could not be vulgar; at first you had almost nothing except not being vulgar. You began with nothing but a hatred; but I knew your hatred was noble, and I know your love would be noble. No; it is not that sort of obvious difficulty at all. We must end here because we have gone round the whole world and thought as far as thinking will go. That is not conceit; it is not a question of knowing everything now, but of being ready to understand anybody at any time. You would not melt into a Regular Guy; you did not dry up into a Superman; and after that you will become a man and understand all men. We must end now, because of all those who have thus understood all things, from the cedar to the hyssop, hardly any (not even Solomon himself) have resisted the temptation to say a last word, to sum it all up, and to say, Vanity of Vanities. Let us, let me at least, resist the temptation, and say, not *Vanitas*, but only *Vale*...Farewell."

John Crake sat down and wrote a long and earnest and delicate letter of thanks, surveying all the thousand things that he had gained in that voyage round the world with that invisible companion. Then he sprang up like a spring released and rushed down the road like a boy freed from school; all the noises of nature seemed to be shouting and cheering him on, for he felt for the first time that he had a body, and it was racing to outstrip his sole.

Before that autumn had turned to winter he was married to Mary Wendover, the lady of the clothes-line; and it is typical of the tail foremost or back-door fashion of his introduction that he never knew her name was Wendover until about a month after he knew it was

Mary. She was apparently a guest in the house of her relative; but
the guest seemed to do all the work while the hosts pursued self-
development. "Very self-development," said Crake, "but I think,
as usual, the Cinderella was the favourite of the fairies." And indeed
she seemed to show a more artistic ardour for pots and pans than they
did for arts; as if the teapot were indeed a familiar goblin or the broom
a benevolent witch's broomstick. After their marriage her creative
concentration increased; and Crake, remembering his own chance
words of encouragement, felt it natural to be infected with the same
fury of efficiency. He wanted to deal with things directly, with his
own hands, as she did; and he announced one day that he had sold
out his business and was going to work a farm he had about ten miles
from the city. She only laughed, and said: "I thought you were already
doing business with realities."

"Why," he cried, "that is out of my celebrated disgraceful speech.
I didn't know...."

"You must have known ladies are allowed to overhear Bisons
eating," she said.

"Well, it shows how little I knew in those days. Business men do
business with unrealities. Only with unrealities. With rubber forests
nobody has seen or ivory from elephants who might be fabulous like
unicorns. I want to cut down a real tree and ride a real horse and
be real."

Indeed, there was a reality in their very romance; and their common
passion went back to its romantic origin. Slight as had been the gesture
of their introduction, it had been active and abrupt. What he had seen
had been a woman wrestling with a rope; and what she had seen had
been a man bounding over a bush; and all their love and life went
with that gallop of bodily vigour and the high gestures of the mastery
of man.

It was about three years later, and, save for the noise of two children
in the old farmhouse, a man would have said that their whole life was
unchanged. He still rode his horses round the farm, and his body was
still young enough to find automatic exultation in the exercise; she
still practised a hundred arts and crafts under the name of
housekeeping, and would have let loose a violent scorn against

anyone who called it drudgery. They both enjoyed to the full the pleasure of doing things well, and there are few pleasures more enduring; and yet a more subtle critic might have said that things were changed. But John Crake could only think of one critic who would have been subtle enough to say it.

Perhaps it was a proof that things were changed that he had thought of that subtle critic at all. But he did now recall that cooler background of friendship, and told himself that she would have understood. Above all, she would not have misunderstood. She would not have been cheap, and supposed that he was merely tired of his wife. In reality, he was not tired in the least. He felt that he wanted her and he had missed her, in spite of having married her. Moreover, there grew upon him a dull pain in the feeling that his wife herself had become sad and estranged. He had seen her staring out of the window on bright summer days; and her face was sadder for the sunlight. Her plunging practicality was often interrupted by her sudden stillness. She liked more and more to be alone. John Crake was no fool, and would have thought nothing of these moods if they had occurred in a moody person. If she had been of the sentimental sort it would not have distressed him much even if he had thought (as he was sometimes inclined to think) that they were somehow connected with personal memories, and even with personal memories of another person. He was shrewd enough to know that romances do very little harm to the romantic. The sort of person for whom lost loves or faded fancies can be stirred by music or turned into minor poetry is generally the sort of person who can indulge them without much danger to the solid loyalties of life. But Mary Crake was not particularly romantic; and certainly the very reverse of sentimental. She had a passion for the practical, for translating thoughts into things. She would no more desire to have a romance without turning it into a reality than to have a recipe without turning it into a dish. She could no more have lived on dreams than she could have dined on a cookery book. Ever since he had seen her wrestling with a clothes-line like an Amazon lassooing a wild horse, he had been affected by her powerful impatience and directness of design. People of that sort do not brood for pleasure. If she was brooding, she was suffering.

He, in his turn, brooded long upon that brooding; pacing up and down the long verandah into which was extended the wide porch of the American farmhouse. All round him was that dreary plain that is the incongruous background of that cheery people, and one straight American road ran up to the very steps of his own porch, a road lined with lean, spidery trees. The road ended with the farm, and it seemed to his sullen eye like the road of destiny, that leads so straight to achievement and disappointment. With an abrupt movement, he turned his back upon it, went into his study, and sat down at his desk. Before he had risen from it he had broken the silence of four years, and written to that long-lost friend and counsellor who had never had a name.

He came out again upon the porch, with his sealed and stamped letter in his hand, and saw that the long road between the thin trees had a black object upon it, the dark angular figure of a man, with a hat tilted over his eyes, so as to show nothing but a sour grin. It was Jackson Drill, the bootlegger; and Crake had an instant overwhelming sense of repugnance. There had been a time when they were the two cynics of Bison City, and seemed to be in a sort of sympathy in their lack of sympathy. It measured the distance that Crake had really travelled along that road of destiny, that the distant sight of Drill was like the sight of a black scorpion. He had long felt that that sort of pessimism was mere poison. The hand that held the letter made an involuntary movement, as if not wishing even the externals of such an understanding to be exposed to such a misunderstanding. The movement, of course, produced the very effect it was meant to avoid.

"Very confidential correspondence, I suppose," said Drill. "Three years after marriage is about the time they start. In fact, old man, I fear it isn't the only confidential correspondence in the house."

Crake said in a very low and restrained voice: "What the devil in hell do you mean?"

Drill laughed with disagreeable agreeableness; for Americans are not afraid to be familiar with their wealthier employers, so far as language is concerned. "Well," he said, "if you have your private correspondence, why shouldn't she? By all accounts, she used to have letters, even in the old days, that you didn't see. That you weren't meant to see."

"Oh, indeed!" said Crake, thoughtfully, and hit the man a crack on his crooked mouth that sent him from the top of the steps to the bottom, and left him spread-eagled on the flat road below. Then Crake turned and entered his own house in so towering a passion that it might have shaken the topmost chimneys and brought them down.

His wife was sitting with her back to him at a writing-desk, reading an old faded letter, and, though he could not see her face, he knew when he first heard her voice that she had been in tears; a terrible and portentous thing in her case.

"Who is that letter from?" he asked, with his voice on a dead level.

She rose and faced him, and her low voice rang out:

"Who are you to talk about letters?" she said. "Who is that letter for?"

Then, after a deadly silence, she added, almost grimly:

"Give me that letter."

"Why should I?" he answered, frowning at her.

"Oh," she replied, almost lightly, "only because it is addressed to me."

And with that he looked across at the old letter she was reading, and saw that it was one of those that he had sent to the same address.

There are thirty-seven morals to this story; but one of them is that it is he who has really gone round the whole world who is anxious to come home; that the end of wisdom is the beginning of life; and that God Himself bowed down to enter a narrow door, in the hour when the Word was made flesh.

SOURCES AND NOTES

The title of each piece follows the number of the page on which it appears in this book, and this in turn is followed by details of its first publication. A few of the stories were subsequently included in anthologies or interspersed in Chesterton's collections of essays; such appearances are not listed here but, where they occur, they can usually be found in John Sullivan's various volumes of bibliography.

Some pieces have been taken from *The Coloured Lands* (London Sheed and Ward, 1938). Most of the copies of this book were destroyed in the war, and it has never been reprinted. These stories are some of Chesterton's earliest attempts at fiction, and cannot be dated more precisely than by the attributions given in the book by Maisie Ward.

11 'Introductory: on Gargoyles' from *The Daily News'*, 16th Jan. 1909 (as 'The Three Temples') □ 17 'A Crazy Tale' from *The Quarto*, vol. 3 (London: Virtue, 1897) □ 23 'Homesick at Home' *c.* 1896 (from *The Coloured Lands*) 27 'Culture and the Light' from *G.K.'s Weekly*, 25th June 1927 □ 29 'A Picture of Tuesday' from *The Quarto*, vol. 1 (London: Virtue, 1896) □ 32 'The Two Taverns' from *G.K.'s Weekly*, 20th Nov. 1926 □ 33 'The Taming of the Nightmare' *c.* 1892 (from *The Coloured Lands*) □ 45 'The Long Bow' from *The Daily News*, 7th Nov. 1908 □ 48 'The Three Dogs' from *G.K.'s Weekly*, 4th Aug. 1928 □ 50 'The Curious Englishman' from *The Daily News*, 1907 □ 53 'A Nightmare' *c.* 1907 (from *The Coloured Lands)* □ 56 'The Giant' from *The Daily News* 31st Oct. 1908 □ 58 'The Tree of Pride' from *The Storyteller*, 1923 □ 59 'A Legend of Saint Francis' from *G.K.'s Weekly*, 9th Oct. 1926 □ 61 'The Angry Street' from *The Daily News*, 25th Jan. 1908, as 'A Somewhat Improbable Story' □ 65 'The Legend of the Sword' from *G.K.'s Weekly*, 15th Sept. 1928 □ 67 'How I Found the Superman' from *The Daily News*, 5th Dec. 1908 □ 70 'Dukes' from *The Daily News*, 30 Oct. 1909 □ 'The Roots of the World' from *The Daily News*, 1907 □ 76 'Chivalry Begins at Home' from *G.K.'s Weekly*, 19th Sept. 1925 □ 78 'The Sword of Wood' from *The Pall Mall Magazine*, Nov. 1913 ❑ 93 'The Dragon at Hide-and-Seek' from *Number Two Joy Street* (Oxford: Blackwell, 1928) □ 99 'The Second Miracle' from *G.K.'s Weekly*, 5th Nov. 1927 □ 101 'The Conversion of an Anarchist' from *The Touchstone*, vol.V, no. 6, Sept. 1919 □ 108 'Concerning Grocers as Gods' from *G.K.'s Weekly*, 11th April, 1925 □ 112 'A Real Discovery: by a would-be discoverer' from *G.K.'s Weekly*, 1st Aug. 1925 □ 117 'The Paradise of Human Fishes' from *G.K.'s Weekly*, 28th March 1925 □ 121 'The Great Amalgamation' from *G.K.'s Weekly*, 19th March 1927 □ 122 'On Secular Education' from *G.K.'s Weekly*, 16th June 1928 □ 124 'A Fish Story' from *G.K.'s Weekly*, 5th Dec. 1925 □ 128 'On Private Property' from *G.K.'s Weekly*, 19th March 1927 □ 130 'The End of Wisdom' from *The Fothergill Omnibus* (London: Eyre and Spottiswood, 1931)

My thanks are due to Alison Bailey and Chris Jackson, without whose assistance many of the stories herein would have remained uncollected; to Aidan Mackey, specialist in Chestertonian rarities, for his kind help and encouragement; to Messrs A.P. Watt Ltd, agents for the Chesterton Estate; and once again to Dorothy Collins.

M.S.